S.CREAM Club

PICK YOUR
YOUR
TH

W9-AGC-908

Now You See Me, Now You Don't!

By Tracey West

To Bonnie Bader: editor, friend,
writing partner, and someone with
a fine appreciation for spookiness—T.W.

For Karen, who taught me, with love
and light, anything is possible—B.D.

Copyright © 2003 by Tracey West. Illustrations © 2003 by
Brian W. Dow. All rights reserved. Published by Grosset & Dunlap,
a division of Penguin Young Readers Group, 345 Hudson Street,
New York, NY 10014. GROSSET & DUNLAP is a trademark of
Penguin Group (USA) Inc. Published simultaneously in Canada.
Printed in the U.S.A.

Library of Congress Cataloging-in-Publication Data is available.

ISBN 0-448-43225-0   A B C D E F G H I J

S.Cream Shop

PICK YOUR PATH

Now You See Me, Now You Don't!

By Tracey West

Illustrated by Brian W. Dow

Grosset & Dunlap • New York

"Happy birthday to you! Happy birthday to you! Happy birthday, dear Amy! Happy birthday to you!"

Amy Izzo tried to smile. The song had started out strong, but most of the voices had started to fade by the last "Happy Birthday." Not Aunt Irene's voice, of course. She got louder and louder as the song went on, and sang the last "you" in a high, rich voice, like an opera singer.

Amy leaned over the lopsided chocolate cake to blow out the candles. Twelve pink candles flickered in a circle around the cake, with a white one in the middle—for luck.

"No so fast, Amy," Aunt Irene said. "You have to make a birthday wish."

Amy sighed. Everybody knew that birthday wishes never came true. What was the point?

Sure, she could make a wish. She could wish to be popular, with lots of friends, so she could have her twelfth birthday party at the movie theater like other kids did, instead of in her boring old kitchen with just her family. She could wish for friends to have sleep over parties with or do homework with.

Amy got lost in the daydream for a bit, then snapped back to reality. Wishing for friends was dumb. If you had friends, you had to think of things to say to them, and laugh at their jokes, and whisper to them when the teacher wasn't looking. Amy wasn't good at any of those things. She was much too shy. No, wishing for friends was useless.

Maybe I should wish for everyone to leave me alone, Amy thought. Now that's a useful wish.

Amy leaned over once more to blow out the candles. But her little brother, Mikey, climbed on top of the table before she could do it.

"Mikey's cake!" Mikey cried. Then he blew out the candles. Tiny drops of toddler drool rained over the chocolate icing.

"Oh, isn't that cute," Mrs. Izzo said. "Mikey thinks it's his birthday!"

Amy sighed again and slumped back into her seat. Her mom thought everything Mikey did was cute.

"That's okay," Amy grumbled. "I didn't need a wish, anyway."

Amy looked around the table. No one seemed to notice her misery. Mikey sat in her mom's lap, shoving cake into his mouth by the handful while her mom wiped icing off of his face. Amy's dad was reading a book that rested on his lap, under the table—but that was normal. Frank Izzo was always reading a book. And Aunt Irene was bustling around the kitchen, pulling plates and forks out of the avocado-green kitchen cabinets.

Aunt Irene cut slices of cake for everyone. Amy's had a Mikey-sized handprint on top. The kitchen was silent while everyone ate their cake. Then Aunt Irene put her fork down with a clatter and beamed at Amy.

"Isn't it about time Amy opened her presents?" she asked.

Now, usually an eleven-year-old girl who had just turned twelve would be very excited about opening presents. But not Amy. She already knew what she would get. Her dad always got her a book. Her mom always got her a new cardigan sweater to replace the one from last year. And Aunt Irene—well, that was another story.

Aunt Irene was everything that Amy wasn't. Aunt Irene was tall, and Amy was medium-sized. Aunt Irene had frizzy red hair, while Amy's was a dull mousy brown and very straight. And Aunt Irene was always loud. When she walked into a room, she got everyone's attention. But Amy was as quiet as a mouse, and no one ever noticed her.

The problem with Aunt Irene's presents is that she was always giving Amy things that were very

Aunt Irene-like instead of Amy-like. Last year, it was a hot pink dress with feathers around the collar. Amy could only imagine what this year's gift would be.

Amy opened up her book and her sweater. Then Aunt Irene handed her a small box wrapped in shiny purple paper. Amy had never received anything small from Aunt Irene before.

"Thank you," Amy said, just a little curious. She tore off the paper and opened the box.

Inside was a smaller box covered in black velvet. Amy lifted the lid.

A necklace rested on a cushion of white silk. Amy had never seen anything like it. A milky-white stone was set in the middle of a silver circle. Strange-looking symbols were engraved all around the circle. The pendant dangled from a thin silver chain.

To her surprise, Amy found that she liked it.

"Thanks, Aunt Irene," she said. "Where did you find it?"

"It's a funny story," her aunt replied. "I was strolling around town one day and came across a little shop—Sebastian Cream's Junk Shop. Have you ever been there?"

"No," Amy replied. She didn't even know it existed.

"Well, I told the shop owner I was looking for

a present for my niece," her aunt continued. "I described you to him, and he said the necklace would be perfect. It's not my style, but I thought you might like it."

"I do," Amy said, giving her aunt a hug.

Later that night, Amy sat on her bed, examining the necklace.

I bet Keesha would like it, too.

Amy sighed again. Keesha had once been Amy's friend—her first friend, and her best friend. They were in class together from kindergarten to second grade. But they hadn't been in the same class for years, and for all that time they hardly spoke to each other. Now they were in the same sixth-grade class, but Amy barely had the courage to say hello to her.

Amy stood up. "Who knows? Maybe I *will* show Keesha," she said aloud. She took the necklace out of its box and walked to the mirror on her closet door.

"Or maybe she'll notice it on her own," Amy said. "After all, it is pretty unusual."

Amy put the chain around her neck. She fastened the clasp.

And then she vanished.

Amy stared into the mirror. Her reflection had completely disappeared!

There must be something wrong with the

mirror! Amy thought.

Amy took a deep breath. She looked down at her body.

She couldn't see a thing. Her legs, her arms—they were gone.

"I'm invisible," Amy whispered.

No, that couldn't be. People just didn't become invisible. It had to have something to do with the necklace. Some kind of trick. Like a hologram or something.

Amy took off the necklace. Immediately, her reflection reappeared in the mirror. The necklace was definitely responsible. But how?

Trembling, Amy sat back down on her bed. She turned the necklace over and over, searching for some kind of answer. She found nothing.

Amy dropped the necklace on her night table and climbed under the covers.

It must be my imagination, she thought. I'll put it on again in the morning, when I'm not so tired.

But Amy didn't sleep well at all, and woke as soon as the first rays of morning sun shone in her room. She quickly sat up. The white stone of the necklace seemed to be staring at her from the night table, like some kind of eye.

Had it all been a dream? There was only one way to find out.

Amy carefully picked up the necklace and walked to the mirror. She put the necklace on— and once again became invisible.

Amy took off the necklace and stared at it, her heart beating fast. She had read enough fantasy books to know that some kinds of jewels were supposed to have magic powers. Could this really be a magic necklace?

"Amy! Time to wake up!" her mother called.

Amy scanned her room for a hiding place. If this really was a magic necklace, she needed to find out more about it. She'd keep it somewhere safe until she got home from school.

Then another thought crept into Amy's mind. A necklace that made you invisible could come in handy at school. She could bring it with her in case of . . . emergency. Like, if it were dodgeball day in gym class. She could put the necklace on, and no more dodge ball . . . just like that!

Amy turned the necklace over in her hand. Did she really have the guts to use it?

If Amy takes the necklace to school, go to page 17.

If Amy leaves the necklace at home, go to page 56.

Continued from page 79

Breaking the stone had freed the Shadow People. Maybe gluing the stone back together would trap them in the necklace once more. It was worth a try. She reached down and scooped up the broken stone.

Amy ran for the door, brushing past some of the shadow people as she went. Their touch felt like ice against her skin.

Amy slammed the door behind her and ran downstairs. Her mom kept the glue in the family computer room. She had to get there—fast.

Amy ran into the computer room, quickly shut the door, and made a beeline for the desk. She grabbed the white bottle of glue and unscrewed the cap.

Suddenly, Amy felt a cold chill. She turned to see the white fog creeping under the door.

You are one of us now, Amy. Don't fight it.

The voices of the shadow people seeped through the door in a sinister whisper. Amy forced herself to turn around and focus on her task. It was her only chance.

The glue stuck to her trembling fingers as she worked, but she did it. The three pieces fit together like a puzzle. There was an airy, wailing sound, and Amy watched in awe as the smoke swirled back into the stone. Then it was silent, and the smoke was gone.

She had done it. She had scared the Shadaw People back in the stone.

Amy stared at the necklace. She imagined what it would be like to be trapped there, like the Shadow People, and shuddered.

There was only one thing to do now. She had to take the necklace back to where it came from— Sebastian Cream's Junk Shop.

Go to page 144.

Continued from page 25

Amy and Billy ran to the left. After a few turns, they found themselves back at Agatha Bleaker-Higgins's drawing room.

"Stop!" Billy cried. "Let's take the silver cube. We might never get another chance."

"Right," Amy agreed, "but we'd better hurry. Once Willard gets out of his office, he's going to come looking for us."

Billy nodded. Amy slid under the rope and picked up the cube. She noticed something she hadn't seen before.

Each side of the cube had a circular pendant in it, except one. There was an empty space where the pendant should go.

"My necklace should fit right in there," Amy realized. "I wonder if that means something."

"Let's try it!" Billy said anxiously.

At Billy's prodding, Amy used the cube to smash open the lock on the box holding the necklace. Then she fit the round pendant into the hole on the side of the cube.

Immediately, the sides of the box sprung open. A bright white light shot out and hit the ceiling. Transfixed, Billy floated off of his feet and entered the light.

"I can see my house!" Billy cried. "And there's my sister! Amy, I'm going home! We did it!"

The light vanished, and the cube snapped shut once again. Amy couldn't believe it. The cube had sent Billy back home!

Amy put the cube back on the desk and removed her necklace from its spot. She put it around her neck, just to see what would happen.

To her surprise, nothing at all happened. She didn't turn invisible.

The necklace must have lost its magic, Amy realized. Now that Billy is home, its job is done.

Amy smiled, happy for her friend. She quickly left the museum and walked down the street, still fingering the necklace. She missed Billy already, but she was glad he was home.

And she'd always have the necklace to remember him by.

THE END

After school, Amy decided to walk downtown to try to find the shop where Aunt Irene had bought the necklace. The shop owner might be able to tell her what the necklace was all about.

Amy walked down tree-lined streets toward Main Street, where most of the stores in Bleaktown were located. She was about to cross the street when something made her stop. There, on the other side of the street, was a gray building as long as a city block.

But that wasn't what got Amy's attention. It was the large front door. Strange symbols were carved into the wood—symbols that looked a lot like the ones on her necklace.

Amy took the necklace out of its box and held it up. They were the same symbols, all right. The building and the necklace must be connected somehow—but how?

She thought about knocking on the door, but what would she say? Maybe she should just peek in a window or something instead.

If Amy decides to snoop around, go to page 49.

If Amy knocks on the door, go to page 94.

It couldn't hurt to bring the necklace to school, Amy reasoned. *Besides, if I leave it here, Mikey will probably find it and ruin it, no matter where I hide it.*

That settled it. When it was time to leave, Amy put the necklace in its box, and put the box in the pocket of her new cardigan sweater.

As Amy walked to school, it seemed as though the box was throbbing in the pocket, almost as though it was alive—and wanted to get out.

It's probably my imagination, Amy considered, trying to reassure herself. But then she thought if the necklace had made her become invisible maybe it had other strange powers, too.

Amy pondered this as she walked to school. Around her, kids walked in groups, laughing and talking. Some boys were tossing a ball back and forth as they ran. None of them seemed to notice Amy. They never did.

Usually, Amy stared at them, wondering what it would be like to be one of them. But today, she didn't even see them. Her brain was practically bursting with thoughts about the necklace.

There had to be a lot of things you could do with an invisible necklace, like the dodgeball-ditching idea she had thought of earlier. She wondered what other people might do if they had an invisible necklace. A bad person might turn invisible and rob a bank or steal a rare treasure from a museum. Her dad would probably use it to stay all night in the library, reading books without anyone bothering him.

But what would Amy do? Her birthday wish popped into her mind:

I wish everyone would leave me alone.

Amy stopped and touched the box in her pocket. If people couldn't see you, they would certainly leave you alone.

Before Amy knew it, she was standing at the front steps of Augustus Bleaker Elementary School. Amy found her classroom and sank into her seat in the back row. She carefully took the box out of her pocket and opened the lid, keeping the box hidden under the desk. The white stone stared back at her.

Amy couldn't concentrate at all that morning. Soon it was time to leave the classroom and go to art class. Amy reluctantly closed the box and put it back in her pocket.

In the art room, Amy found her easel. They were learning how to paint bowls of fruit. Amy walked to the supply cabinet to pick out a paintbrush when she felt a tap on her shoulder.

"Hi, Amy!"

Amy turned. It was Keesha.

"Hi," Amy said. The word came out in a whisper.

"You should sit with us at lunch today," Keesha said. "I know you usually sit by yourself, but that's silly."

"Uh, I, uh," Amy stammered. Keesha sat with some of the most popular girls in sixth grade. Amy's throat tightened as she thought about sitting with those girls. They'd expect her to talk, and be funny. She couldn't do it. She just couldn't. She wanted desperately to explain all this to Keesha, but the words just didn't come.

"Great! See you at lunch," Keesha said. Then she turned and walked away.

Amy felt the necklace throb in her pocket. A thought struck her. She could use the necklace to turn invisible at lunchtime. Keesha would never find her.

At the same time, Amy realized how silly she sounded. All she had to do was talk to Keesha and explain how she felt. That couldn't be so hard—could it?

If Amy decides to use the necklace at lunch, go to page 33.

If Amy finds the courage to talk to Keesha, go to page 41.

Amy's self-preservation instinct kicked in. She let go of the chain and tore into the hallway. To her left, she saw another door. She pushed through it and ran to the street outside.

Amy kept running until she couldn't run anymore. She leaned against a mailbox, breathing hard.

It's over, she thought, relief sweeping over her body. I don't have to worry about the necklace anymore.

Her thought had barely finished when the blue afternoon sky suddenly turned dark. A thunderous sound rumbled through Bleaktown, causing the leaves on the trees to quake and the ground to tremble.

Amy expected rain to fall, but the grayness overhead didn't look like clouds. It looked more like a flat gray sheet.

"Like a shadow," Amy whispered, her blood running cold.

Slowly, people emerged from the houses around Amy, curious and scared at the same time. As they watched the sky, the giant figure of a woman appeared, towering over the town. Her white-blond hair streamed behind her. Her cold blue eyes flashed with lightning.

"Diamanda!" Amy cried.

Amy had never seen anything like it. Diamanda looked terrifying and indestructible.

I should never have left the stone behind, Amy though bitterly.

Overhead, Diamanda grinned a terrible, wicked grin.

"Bleaktown, welcome to your future!" She boomed. "Welcome to the Shadow World!"

THE END

Continued from page 73

"It still feels like stealing," Amy said. "Why don't I use my necklace instead? I can turn invisible and get a closer look at it."

Billy shrugged. "Fine with me. Just make it quick, okay?"

Amy slipped the necklace around her neck. Then, invisible, she crawled under the velvet rope and approached the desk. She picked up the cube and examined it.

The cube was heavy, and Amy guessed it must be made of solid silver. On each side of the cube was embedded a circular pendant. Each pendant had symbols carved around the edges and a white stone in the center—just like her necklace.

"I think I found something!" Amy called to Billy, then she clasped her hand over her mouth. Just because she couldn't be seen didn't mean that someone couldn't hear her.

But she was too late. A man in a rumpled brown suit turned the corner and entered the display area. Billy vanished just in time, but Amy froze, the cube still in her hands. The man gasped when he saw the cube, which to him seemed to be floating in midair.

"My heavens!" he cried.

Amy quickly put down the cube. She started to run, but tripped over the velvet rope. The jolt knocked the clasp loose, and the necklace clattered to the floor. Amy became visible again.

"What is going on here?" the man asked. He reached down and helped Amy to her feet.

Too late, Amy realized the necklace was still on the floor. She bent down to pick it up, but the man beat her to it.

"My goodness," he said, his eyes growing wide. "Can it be? What an amazing discovery."

He turned to Amy. "Who are you?" he asked. "Where did you get this?"

"My name's Amy," she replied bravely. "And that is my birthday present. May I have it back, please?"

"Well, Amy, my name is Professor Marcus Willard," he said. "And I'm afraid I can't give this back to you. Do you know what this is?"

"It's my necklace," she said, "and I want it back."

Professor Willard clicked his tongue. "No, no, I'm afraid that won't do. Please come to my office. We'll discuss this further."

Amy followed the professor through the twisting hallways. Billy was connected to that necklace, and she wasn't about to let it out of her sight.

"I'm still here," Billy whispered in her ear. "I

just haven't materialized all the way. Don't let him take it!"

"I won't," Amy whispered back.

Finally they reached Willard's cluttered office. Books and papers littered nearly every inch of space. Willard tossed some books off of a chair and beckoned for Amy to sit down. Then he went to his shelf and pulled out an old book bound in red leather.

"This is the journal of Agatha Bleaker-Higgins," he said. "In it, she describes a necklace that can turn the wearer invisible. No one has ever found it—until today, that is. I saw you appear before my eyes. This is the necklace."

Amy bit her lip. She had no idea what Willard planned to do with the necklace. She had to make sure Billy was safe.

"It's more than that," Amy said. "The necklace is important. I'm trying to help somebody and I need it. Please give it back!"

Professor Willard clicked his tongue. "Oh no," he said. "The necklace is too important to trust to a little girl. If you won't help me, I'll figure it out for myself!"

Professor Willard stood up. He clasped the necklace around his own neck.

Nothing happened.

"But that's impossible," he said. "I...I saw you

appear before my eyes. I know I did."

Amy didn't understand why the necklace hadn't worked for the professor, but she was glad. Maybe he would give it back to her now.

"You must be seeing things." Amy said.

Professor Willard scowled. He put the necklace in a wooden box on his desk and locked the box with a key. Then he walked to the door.

"I'm going to leave you and the necklace in here for safekeeping," he said. "Please understand. This discovery is too important to ignore!"

He closed the door, and Amy heard him lock it. Billy materialized fully in front of her.

"What are we going to do now?" Amy asked.

"First we need to get out of this room," Billy said. He showed Amy how to jiggle the lock with a paper opener from Professor Willard's desk. Amy grabbed the box holding the necklace and then they both ran out into the hallway.

But Amy had no idea where they were. The hallway extended to the left and right, then ended in another turn on both sides.

"Which way should we go?" Amy wondered.

If Amy and Billy go to the left, go to page 14.

If Amy and Billy go to the right, go to page 36.

Continued from page 52

Amy's gut told her to run, to save herself, but something in her wouldn't let her leave the necklace behind. She was still struggling with the chain when two of the shadow people grabbed her arms—a teenage girl and the boy named Adam.

"Who are you?" Diamanda asked.

"I—I brought you the invisibility talisman," Amy bluffed. "It's what you want, isn't it?"

Diamanda's eyes rested on the necklace. She reached out and grabbed it. It came right off the nail.

"You're lying," Diamanda said. "But it's no matter. We have all three talismans. The future of Bleaktown is in our hands!"

The members of the Shadow Society applauded. The old man stepped behind Amy and locked the library doors.

"You're letting her stay?" Adam asked. "But Mother, we don't know who she is."

Diamanda shrugged. "We must keep an eye on her while we perform the spell. The time is right. We must act now."

Diamanda placed Amy's necklace on the pedestal with the other talismans. Adam and the teenage girl guided Amy to a chair in the corner and pushed her down. Then they rejoined the other nine members of the society, forming a circle around the pedestal.

Diamanda walked to one of the bookshelves and came back holding an old leather-bound book. She searched through the pages and then stopped, holding the book in front of her.

"I will read the words of the spell," she said. "When I am finished, Bleaktown will be plunged into the Shadow World forever!"

Amy's mind raced. These people had to be crazy—but then again, she knew that her necklace was definitely magic. What if they weren't crazy? Then Bleaktown was in big trouble.

And Amy was the only one who could stop it. But what could she do?

If Amy decides to watch to see if the spell really works, go to page 106.

If Amy makes a move to stop the Shadow Society, go to page 136.

continued from page 110

"Isn't it cheating to steal the answers?" Amy asked weakly.

"Not really," Shelby answered. "Mr. Moore makes his tests too hard. He can't expect anybody to pass them! We have to take matters into our own hands."

"Shelby has a point," Keesha said slowly. "It's really Mr. Moore's fault, in a way."

"Okay," Amy said reluctantly. "Let's do it."

Shelby devised a plan. Mr. Moore kept all of his important papers in his briefcase next to his desk. During lunch the next day, Shelby and Deandra would distract Mr. Moore while he ate at his desk. Then Amy would put on the necklace, open the briefcase, and take out the test answers.

"It's Amy's necklace, so she should be the one to do it," Shelby reasoned.

The next day, the girls met at a table in the corner of the lunchroom. Shelby and Keesha munched on sandwiches, but Amy couldn't eat a bite. Then Shelby led them out of the lunchroom to Mr. Moore's room.

"Now, Amy," Shelby demanded.

Amy put the necklace on and turned invisible. Shelby and Keesha walked inside first.

"Mr. Moore, we have a question about the Social Studies project," Amy heard Shelby say.

Amy took a deep breath and walked into the room. She spotted the briefcase under Mr. Moore's desk on the floor. Amy quietly walked to the desk, knelt down, and slid the briefcase toward her. She bent down to lift up the hinged lock.

Then the necklace swung out and the stone caught on the lock. Amy pulled at the chain, hoping it would come loose.

Instead, it snapped, turning Amy visible again.

"Oh no!" Amy cried. She couldn't help herself.

Mr. Moore's stern face peered over his desk.

"Amy Izzo! What are you doing in my briefcase?" he asked.

Amy didn't know what to say. She was practically sitting on top of the open briefcase.

"Do you girls know anything about this?" he asked Shelby and Keesha.

"No sir," Shelby said. "I'm as shocked as you are."

Keesha flashed Amy an apologetic look.

Mr. Moore walked around the desk. He picked up the briefcase and snapped it shut. Amy cringed as she heard the necklace shatter.

"You are in big trouble, young lady," Mr. Moore said angrily. "What have you got to say for yourself?"

Amy felt like crying. She had no explanation. No necklace. And once again, no friends.

Amy just shrugged. What could she say? She'd probably get detention for this. Or worse.

This has been the worst birthday present ever! Amy thought.

THE END

"All right, we'll face the bank," Amy said reluctantly. "I guess if it's the wrong way, we can always try it again."

Amy brought out the talismans from the shed, while James followed the directions in the book to draw a circle in the dirt. They placed the talismans on the ground inside the circle. Then James read aloud the chant from the book. The words sounded like they belonged to some strange language.

Suddenly, the three talismans burst into flame. Amy jumped back. The flames grew higher and higher.

Amy and James watched, stunned, as a creature stepped from the flames. It looked like a cross between a man and a bull. Its skin was as white as the stone on the talisman of Invisibility, its eyes were as black as the talisman of Power, and when it opened its mouth, it spewed out a red flame the color of the talisman of Transportation.

"Uh, I guess we were facing the wrong way," James whispered to Amy.

"Who dares to disturb the keeper of the talismans?" the creature bellowed.

"We-we didn't mean to," Amy said, her voice trembling.

"Yeah," James added. "We were just trying to destroy the talismans."

"DESTROY THE TALISMANS?" The keeper's voice sounded like a lion's roar. "THEN YOU WILL FEEL MY WRATH! I WILL HUNT YOU TO THE END OF YOUR DAYS!"

"Come on!" James yelled. He grabbed Amy's arm, and they took off running down Amy's driveway.

Amy was too scared to look behind her, but she could feel the keeper's evil presence behind them.

"What do we do now?" Amy asked James.

"Keep running!" James said. "He's got to get tired sometime."

Maybe he will, Amy thought as she tore down the street. *Or maybe we'll get tired first . . .*

THE END

Amy wanted to walk right up to Keesha and tell her how she felt. But she stood by the supply cabinet, frozen. Soon she heard the art teacher's voice.

"Come on, Amy," she said cheerfully. "It's kumquat time!"

Amy tried to focus on painting her kumquat, but all she could think about was the necklace. By the time class was over, Amy had made up her mind to use it.

I'll just try it, Amy thought. *If anything weird happens, I can always take the necklace off.*

When the bell rang, Amy darted out of the room and slipped into the girls' room down the hall. It was empty. She slipped into a stall, just to be safe, and took the necklace out of its box.

"Here goes," Amy whispered. She clasped the necklace around her neck.

Amy vanished instantly. She wondered at how simple it seemed. There were no flashing lights, no mysterious music, just—poof! Invisibility.

Amy waited for the next bell to ring before she stepped out of the bathroom. The halls were empty, but it didn't matter anyway, did it? No one could see her!

Amy's heart beat faster as she walked through the hall. What now? She could do anything she wanted, couldn't she? She thought about doing cartwheels down the hallway, just for fun, but she wasn't very good at them.

Then her stomach rumbled, and Amy realized that she was hungry. Her lunch was sitting in a paper bag in the closet in her classroom. If she wanted to eat, she'd have to go get it.

Amy walked to her room and peeked inside. There was her teacher, Mr. Moore, grading papers at his desk. Amy took a deep breath, then stepped inside the door.

The floorboard underneath her foot creaked. Mr. Moore looked up for a second, shrugged, and then returned to his work.

So he could hear her. Amy took careful steps now, making sure to keep quiet.

Luckily, the closet door was open. Amy stepped in and found her lunch bag. She almost stepped out of the closet when a thought struck her: Wouldn't Mr. Moore be suspicious of a floating lunch bag? She tried tucking the lunch bag under her sweater.

It worked! The bag disappeared. Amy walked out of the classroom, and then, because it was a beautiful day and she was feeling bold, decided to eat outside on the front lawn.

Amy had always wanted to eat outside, but it was against the rules. She found a spot under a shady tree and congratulated herself for being so brave. It wasn't the same as robbing a bank or anything, but to Amy, it felt pretty daring.

As Amy sat down, she felt a chill creep through her body. She had a strange feeling that someone was watching her.

She looked up. A boy was standing there, staring straight at her.

Amy frantically touched her neck to see if the necklace was there. It was. Amy checked her arms and legs. Still invisible. So how could this boy see her?

"Hi," he said, smiling. "My name is Adam."

Amy gasped. The boy smiling at her was not a solid, flesh-and-blood boy. He was oddly transparent, like a character projected on a movie screen. Quickly, she took off the necklace.

The boy disappeared, and Amy was visible again. She stared at the necklace in her hands. Things were getting a little too weird.

If Amy tries to return the necklace to the Scream Shop, go to page 16.

If Amy decides to experiment more with the necklace at home, go to page 53.

continued from page 25

Amy and Billy ran to the right—and right into Professor Willard. He was flanked by three stern-looking men in business suits. Billy quickly disappeared.

"There you are, little girl," the professor said, smiling a fake smile. "I see you've brought me the necklace. How nice of you."

Amy scowled as Willard took the box from her. He unlocked it and took out the necklace.

"Willard, you've been talking about this necklace for years," one of the men said. "Are we really supposed to believe this preposterous story?"

"Just watch," Willard said, his eyes gleaming.

Before Amy could stop him, he slipped the necklace around her neck. She vanished in an instant.

The men gasped.

"Willard, that's incredible!" said another. "How does it work?"

"I'm not sure," Professor Willard said. "And for some reason, it only seems to work with the girl."

That's when Amy's nightmare began. The museum directors notified her parents, who were completely shocked. They tried to protect Amy from the public, but when word got out, her house was swamped with TV cameras every day.

Everyone wanted to see "Amy the Invisible Girl." Amy tried going on a few talk shows, just to satisfy people's curiosity, but it only got worse.

Then the government stepped in. They took Amy to a top-secret test facility, where she was tested and poked and prodded every day.

Billy was the only bright spot in her life. Whenever he could, he materialized nearby. But it made Amy sad to think that he would never get back to his own time.

Amy remembered the night it all started, when she had tried to make her birthday wish. All she had wanted was to be left alone.

"I was right," Amy muttered, as the government scientists came to take another X-ray. "Birthday wishes never do come true!"

THE END

Continued from page 98

Amy decided that following the boy might be her best chance for escape. She stepped behind the pillar. The boy grabbed her arm and pulled her down.

"There's a crawl space in here," he said. "It's a way out."

The boy removed a metal grate about three feet square from the wall and crawled inside. Amy crept in behind him. She followed him through the narrow space to another grate, directly underneath them. The boy removed that and jumped down.

"Come on!" he urged her. "It's not far."

Amy's sneakers thudded against concrete as she jumped down to the floor. He had led them into the basement.

As her eyes adjusted to the dim light, Amy got a good look at him. To her surprise, she recognized him from her class—it was James Simms, a new kid.

"I saw that lady push you into your seat," James said. "You don't look like one of them. Are you a spy, too?"

"A spy?" Amy replied. "No, not exactly. I have this necklace, and I wanted to find out more about it."

James nodded. "That's how it started with the rest of them, too. Diamanda located them all and got them to join her Shadow Society."

"I'm really confused," Amy said. "What's going on? Are they really trying to transport Bleaktown somewhere else?"

James nodded. He pulled a photograph from his pocket and gave it to Amy. It was a young man with black hair like James's.

"That's my uncle Marshall," he said. "He's been onto the whole thing from the beginning."

"What whole thing?" Amy asked, exasperated.

"I'm not exactly sure," James said. "It's like Diamanda said. There were these ancient talismans. Then, a long time ago, a secret society formed called the Shadow People. They made copies of the talismans. The talismans have powers, but I guess no one thought of combining their powers until Diamanda came along. She has this crazy idea that modern society is bad—stuff like video games and movies and computers. She wants to take Bleaktown into another dimension to keep it safe."

"That is a crazy idea," Amy agreed. "Do you think she can really do it?"

James nodded. "My uncle thinks so. He's like an expert on this stuff."

"So why doesn't he stop them?" Amy asked.

James's face clouded. "My uncle disappeared three days ago. He was spying on Diamanda, trying to stop her. I think they've kidnapped him. But I'm going to find him."

Amy was impressed. James was the same age as she was, but he sounded a lot braver.

"I can get you out of here if you want," James said. "Unless you want to stay and help me find Uncle Marshall."

Amy wasn't sure what to say. How could she possibly help James?

Then she remembered the necklace. Being invisible could come in handy when you were sneaking around someplace you weren't supposed to be. Maybe she could help, after all. But could she be as brave as James?

Continued on page 127

Continued from page 19

Amy suddenly realized how crazy she sounded. She actually wanted to turn invisible to avoid Keesha. She and Keesha learned how to ride bicycles together. They suffered through chicken pox at the same time. And now Amy was afraid to talk to her.

Amy walked up to Keesha's easel and tapped her friend on the shoulder.

"Thanks for asking me to eat lunch with you," she said. "I'd like to. It's just that . . . I don't really know those other girls."

Keesha smiled. "I forgot how shy you were, Amy," she said. "Tell you what. Why don't we hang out after school instead?"

Amy smiled back, relieved. "Yeah. That'd be great."

When the last school bell rang, Amy found Keesha waiting for her on the school's front steps.

"Can we go to your house?" Keesha asked. "I'd love to escape from my brothers for an afternoon."

"Are you sure?" Amy asked. "I've got Mikey, remember?"

Keesha giggled. "Mikey's a cute little kid. You're lucky you don't have four big dorky brothers who play football in the living room and blast their stereos all day."

Amy shrugged. She had always thought Keesha's brothers were fun to be around. At least they didn't always ruin everything, like Mikey did.

The girls talked the whole walk home, and it almost felt like old times again to Amy. Amy's mom seemed happy and surprised to see Keesha. She let Amy and Keesha go up to Amy's room without even asking Amy to play with Mikey for a while.

"Your room looks just like always," Keesha said. "Remember when we made a fort out of your bed?"

"Yeah, and then my dad put on a Halloween mask and scared us," Amy fell back on the bed, giggling.

The necklace slipped right out of her pocket. Keesha picked up the box.

"What's this?" she asked, opening the lid.

"It's nothing," Amy said quickly. "Just a necklace I got for my birthday."

"It is so pretty!" Keesha exclaimed. She held the chain up against her neck. The white stone gleamed brightly against her dark skin. "Can I try it on?"

"That's not such a good idea," Amy said, panicking. "The clasp is broken, and—"

"It works just fine, silly," Keesha said, attaching the clasp.

And then she vanished.

Amy was speechless. It was one thing turning invisible yourself, but seeing someone else turn invisible was really creepy.

Then a scream came from the empty space where Keesha was supposed to be standing.

"It's okay, Keesha," Amy said. "Take the necklace off!"

A few seconds later, Keesha became visible again. She sank down on the bed, shaking.

"I turned . . . I turned . . ." Keesha couldn't get the words out.

"You turned invisible," Amy said. "I know. It happened to me, too."

Mrs. Izzo's head peeked in the door. "Are you girls all right?"

"Fine, Mom," Amy said quickly. "We were just remembering that time Dad scared us."

Amy's mom smiled. "It's nice to see you two together again." Then she headed back downstairs.

Keesha was a little calmer now. She stared at the necklace in her hands.

"This is big, Amy," she said. "B-I-G. We've got to tell somebody!"

Amy frowned. "I'm not sure if that's such a great idea," she said.

"Come on," Keesha said. "Let's show it to Shelby. She'll just die!"

Amy's frowns grew deeper. Shelby Grisham was one of the most popular girls in sixth grade, and one of Keesha's new friends. Amy had never liked Shelby much.

"Please, Amy," Keesha said. "Think of how much fun we can have with this!"

Continued on page 109.

Amy had a good feeling about Billy. Sure, he was see-through and everything, but he seemed really nice. And there was something strangely familiar about him. Amy couldn't quite put her finger on it.

"I'll help you," Amy decided. "But what do you think I can do?"

"I'm not sure," Billy admitted. "But there must be a reason why I can appear near you. I think it's because of the symbols on your necklace and my coin. Maybe if we can figure out what they mean, we can figure out how to get me back."

"That makes sense," Amy said. "But I don't know much about the necklace. My Aunt Irene gave it to me for my birthday yesterday."

Billy suddenly got a sad look on his face. "Irene," he said. "That's my sister's name. Only I haven't seen her since . . ."

Amy felt sorry for Billy. She wasn't sure how long he had been trapped in the Shadow World, but from the looks of his old-fashioned clothes, it had probably been a long time. Amy found herself determined to help Billy, no matter what she had to do.

Amy tried to think. There had to be some way

to find out what the symbols meant. She thought of her dad, his nose always in a book. Maybe that was the answer.

"My school has a really big library," Amy said. "There are lots of books on ancient civilizations and stuff. Maybe we can find out something about the symbols there."

"That could work," Billy said, "but I was thinking of something else. After I found my lucky coin, my sister and I went to the Bleaktown Museum. I saw something there that had the symbols on it. I wanted to go back and investigate it, but I disappeared into the Shadow World before I had the chance. I was thinking that if you bring the necklace there, I might be able to materialize there with you and check it out."

That sounded reasonable to Amy. Still, she thought, it couldn't hurt to check the library first. Even if they found the symbols on something at the museum, they still wouldn't know what the symbols meant.

If Amy and Billy go to the school library, go to page 66.

If Amy and Billy go to the Bleaktown Museum, go to page 71.

Amy was too frightened to follow the boy. Instead, she kept shuffling along with the rest of the people in gray.

They left the auditorium and climbed up a long staircase that led to the roof of the building. The crowd had formed a circle again, with Diamanda in the center.

"I was just informed that our one hundredth member arrived today," Diamanda announced. "That means we have the exact number we need. Let's begin the chant."

The people in gray began chanting in a strange language. At first, all Amy could do was watch. But as the chanting grew louder, Amy felt compelled to join in. Whatever strange power the talismans had was sweeping her up along with it.

Our one hundredth member . . . Amy's heart sank when she realized that Diamanda had been talking about her. If she hadn't knocked on the door and followed the group to the roof, none of this would be happening.

Suddenly, a thick gray fog began to rise from their feet. The fog swirled around them, expanding until it grew higher and higher and wider and wider. Soon the blue sky and bright sun were blocked from view.

The fog had become solid, like a thick gray blanket. To Amy, it looked as though the whole town of Bleaktown had been sealed inside a dark box.

Then, without warning, a tremendous thunder-clap boomed. Amy could feel her body tremble from the vibrations. Diamanda raised her arms over her head, smiling, and looked up to the dead gray sky.

"We have done it!" Diamanda cried trium-phantly. "Bleaktown has been plunged into the Shadow World!"

THE END

Amy didn't feel quite brave enough to knock on the front door quite yet. She walked down the length of the building, looking for a window at her level, but they were all too high.

Behind the building was a narrow alleyway back by a tall, brick fence. Amy turned into the alley. There were no windows, as far as she could see, but there was an old-looking door. Amy gently pushed on it and found that it wasn't locked.

For some reason she couldn't quite understand, the decision to step inside that door overwhelmed her. Was she really that desperate to find out about the necklace?

The necklace, Amy realized. *I can use the necklace to become invisible. If someone is inside, they won't see me.*

Amy slipped the necklace on and slowly pushed open the door. She found herself inside a dim hallway. Amy could see the entrance to a room at the end of a hall and she heard the murmur of voices as well. Someone was there.

Amy carefully crept down the hall, trying not to make a noise. When she reached the room entrance, she peeked around the corner.

Nine people dressed in gray were sitting in a circle in what looked like some kind of library. One of them was the boy, Adam, who had appeared before Amy at the school earlier. A tall woman with white-blond hair was talking.

"The Shadow Society has never been closer to our goal," she was saying. "We have two of the talismans we need in our possession."

The woman pointed to a skinny pedestal in the center of the circle. Two necklaces rested there. They looked a lot like Amy's necklace, except one had a red stone in the center, and the other had a black stone in the center. Amy wasn't sure, but she thought the symbols carved into the silver might be different, too.

"We have the talisman of Transportation and the talisman of Power," the woman continued. "All we need to complete our task is the talisman of Invisibility."

"I almost located it today, Mother," said Adam. "I used the transportation talisman and saw a girl with it. But then she vanished."

Amy stifled a gasp. Adam was talking about her! Her necklace must be the talisman of Invisibility the woman had mentioned.

One of the nine, a man with white hair, spoke up. "Diamanda, will the three talismans really help us achieve our goal? Will we really be able to plunge Bleaktown into the Shadow World?"

The blond-haired woman smiled. "The ancient texts are not wrong," Diamanda said. "With the combined energy of the three talismans, we can bring Bleaktown into the shadow world and escape the evils of modern society forever!"

"No more video games," said the old man.

"Or violent movies," said another.

"Once we are in the Shadow world, we will take power," Diamanda said. "The future of Bleaktown is in our hands."

Amy felt a chill at Diamanda's words. Sure, she wasn't crazy about those video games where people blew each other's heads off, but the idea of Bleaktown being plunged into some kind of shadow world didn't sound like the answer to that problem. It sounded way creepy.

Amy grasped the stone around her necklace.

They need my necklace to finish their plan, she realized. I have to make sure they never get it!

Amy quickly turned to leave the room, but the necklace chain caught on a nail sticking out of the door frame. Before Amy could stop it, the chain snapped off, and, in an instant, she became visible.

A cry rose from the circle, and the nine members of the Shadow Society rose from their seats.

"It's the girl I saw earlier!" Adam shouted.

"Stop her!" cried Diamanda. "She has the invisibility talisman!"

Amy struggled to release the talisman from the nail. She couldn't let them get ahold of it.

It seemed to Amy that all nine people got up at once and charged after her. She had a microsecond to consider her options.

She could leave now, and leave the necklace behind. The shadow people were probably crazy, anyway. All that talk about a Shadow World was probably nonsense.

Or she could keep trying until she got the necklace loose. It might be the only way to save Bleaktown.

If Amy leaves the necklace behind, go to page 20.

If Amy keeps trying to get the necklace loose, go to page 26.

Continued from page 35

Amy quickly ate her lunch and managed to sneak back into the building without anyone noticing.

That's funny, she thought. *Even when I'm not invisible, nobody sees me.*

For the rest of the day, Amy thought about the necklace—and the ghostly boy named Adam. What did a see-through boy have to do with the necklace? Amy liked being invisible, but being spooked by ghosts—if that's what Adam was—was another thing altogether.

Amy kept the necklace on her lap during class. She stared at the strange symbols carved into the silver circle. They must have something to do with the power of the necklace. If she could figure out what the symbols meant, she might be able to figure out how to use the necklace, or even figure out who Adam was. The thought intrigued her.

When school was done, Amy put the necklace back in her pocket. She promised herself that she wouldn't put it on again until she knew more about it.

Amy wanted more than anything to concentrate on the necklace when she got home, but her mom cornered her as soon as she walked through the door.

"I'd like you to do your homework now, Amy, " Mrs. Izzo said. "I'll be cooking dinner soon, and I could use some help with Mikey."

Of course, Amy sighed. Why should she have any time to herself? Mikey always came first.

So Amy finished three pages of math homework, played a zillion games of peek-a-boo with her brother, and ate a supper of tuna casserole and leftover birthday cake before she could even think about the necklace again.

After the dishes were done, she slipped into the family computer room, where her dad kept all his books. She grabbed *Lord of the Rings*, because that was about a magic jewel, and a thick encylopedia-like book called *A Dictionary of Magic Symbols*.

Amy took both books up to her room, closed the door, and began reading. She read for two hours. The ring in the *Lord of the Rings* made you invisible, but Amy couldn't see what hobbits or wizards had to do with her necklace. The book of symbols wasn't much help, either. Frustrated, she pushed the books to the floor.

Amy stood up and walked to the mirror. She held up the necklace and studied it.

Had she really seen a ghostly boy on the school lawn? Maybe it was a real kid, and her eyes were playing tricks on her. There was only one way to find out.

Forgetting her promise to herself, Amy slipped the necklace on again and watched her reflection disappear in the mirror. Then she slowly turned in a circle, looking for signs of a ghostly boy. Nothing.

Amy faced the mirror again. Now, there was a reflection staring back at her.

It was Adam!

"Aaaargh!" Amy screamed.

If Amy talks to Adam, go to page 60.

If Amy takes off the necklace and stomps on it,

go to page 78.

Continued from page 11

At the last second, Amy shoved the box under her mattress. She didn't want to fool around with the necklace at school until she knew more about it.

For the rest of the day, Amy felt as though she had left her brain back at home with her necklace. It was all she could think about. While her teacher, Mr. Moore, droned on about long division, Amy kept imagining where the necklace had come from. She had read enough books from her dad's library to make a guess.

It might have been enchanted by a powerful wizard. Or maybe a beautiful princess had used it to escape from her wicked parents. Or it might have come from the treasure horde of a tremendous dragon and then stolen by a clever thief.

By the end of the day, Amy's mind was so full of wizards and princesses and dragons that she wasn't paying attention to much else. On the way home, she thudded into a hard object, and her books spilled onto the sidewalk. Amy bent down to pick them up when she heard a nasty voice above her.

"Watch where you're going!"

Amy's heart sank when she realized the hard

object she had thudded into had been none other than David Pierson, a seventh-grader and the biggest bully at August Bleaker Elementary School.

"Sorry," Amy muttered. She reached for her math book, but David scooped it up first.

"If you want it, go get it!" David taunted. Then he threw the book across the street. It landed in the gutter. David and his friends burst out laughing.

Amy's cheeks burned red. She wanted to fight back, but what was the use? Instead, she stomped across the street, picked up her book, and headed home.

Amy's eyes stung with tears as she climbed up to her room and flung herself on her bed.

"Stupid David," she muttered.

"What's wrong?" a friendly voice asked.

Amy sat up. There was a boy in her room. At least, she thought it was a boy.

The boy was see-through, like a projection on a movie screen. He seemed to flicker in and out of view. He wore a green cap on his bright red hair. He had a freckled face, and wore jeans and a green button-down shirt.

Amy's first thought was to scream for her mother, but something held her back.

"Who are you?" Amy asked, her voice trembling. "How did you get here?"

The boy lifted up his hat and scratched his head.

"I'm Billy," he said. "And I'm not sure how I got here at all."

Amy began to feel sorry for the boy. He looked lost and confused.

"I don't understand," she said. "Why are you all . . . see-through?"

Billy sighed. "That's because I'm in the Shadow World. I've been here for years." He reached into his pants pocket and pulled out an old-looking coin.

"It all started when I found this," he said.

Amy looked at the coin. It was covered with strange symbols—just like the ones on her necklace! Excited, Amy took the necklace out from under her mattress and showed it to Billy.

"My necklace has symbols just like your coin," she said.

Billy let out a low whistle. "What do you know? Maybe that's why I can appear in your world. I haven't been here in such a long time," he said.

Billy looked closely at the necklace. "What kind of place is the Shadow World?" Amy asked. She'd never heard of anything like it before.

Billy's face clouded. "It's not a very nice place, that's for sure," he said. Then he leaned over and looked closely at the necklace.

"It can't be a coincidence that your necklace and my coin have the same symbols," he said. "Maybe . . ." he said. "Maybe you can help me escape from this shadow world I'm trapped in. Will you help me?"

Amy wasn't sure what to do. Billy seemed nice enough—but then again, he looked a lot like a ghost. Could she trust him?

If Amy agrees to help Billy, go to page 45.

If Amy refuses to help Billy, go to page 124.

Continued from page 55

Amy turned around. Adam was standing behind her, just as transparent as before. He looked about Amy's age. His brown hair was neatly combed, and he wore a pair of very blue jeans and a white button-down shirt with short sleeves. Amy thought he kind of looked like the older brother on that old black-and-white Leave It to Beaver show her mom watched on TV. Somehow, that made him less scary.

Amy found her courage. "Who are you?" she asked.

"I told you," he said. "My name's Adam."

His voice sounded friendly, although it did sound like he was talking through a tunnel.

"I guess, I mean—what are you, exactly?" Amy asked.

Adam laughed. "I'm a boy. Can't you tell?"

Amy forgot she was scared. This boy was more annoying than scary.

"No, I mean, why do you appear when I put on the necklace? And how can you see me?" she asked.

Adam reached into his shirt and pulled out a chain that he wore around his neck. Dangling from the chain was what looked like an old coin.

It had a hole in the middle.

"Your necklace is magic," he said. "Just like my lucky coin. It's fun to turn invisible, isn't it?"

It wasn't exactly the answer Amy was looking for, but she was intrigued.

"I haven't done it a lot," Amy said. "It feels a little scary. And then you showed up—"

"Don't be a worrywart!" Adam said. "Have fun being invisible. It's what you want, isn't it?"

Amy's mind filled with questions to ask Adam, but she didn't get the chance. The boy disappeared before her eyes. Amy took off the necklace and sat on her bed.

She thought about what to do. Adam really wasn't scary, once you talked to him. And he said that being invisible was fun. That was true. Amy remembered how free she felt, sneaking out of school to eat outside. Maybe Adam was right. Maybe she should stop being a worrywart.

The next morning, Amy ducked behind a tree a few yards from her house and put on the necklace. She tucked her books and her lunch bag under her sweater so they wouldn't attract any attention. Then she walked to school, invisible the whole way.

After a few blocks, Amy saw Keesha walking with some of her friends. Normally, Amy would have hid behind a tree to avoid them. But now she walked right up to them and walked in step with the group.

"I can't believe all that homework we had last night," Keesha was saying.

"Yeah, Mr. Moore must think we have, like, no lives!" one of the girls replied.

When they reached the school, Amy hid behind a tree and took off the necklace. This invisibility thing was working out great.

All morning, Amy planned how to use the necklace next. It was Tuesday, which meant they had gym class. Amy hated gym. She always got picked last for every team.

She'd have to be visible when class started, when the gym teacher took attendance, Amy reasoned. After that, she could sneak behind the bleachers and turn invisible. No one would even notice she was gone.

Amy trembled nervously when it came time for gym. Could she really go through with her plan? First things first. She'd have to change into her gym clothes.

Amy followed the girls into the locker room. Amy's locker was in the back corner, away from the other girls. She liked it like that. Amy sat on the bench and slipped off her left shoe. Her white ankle sock got caught in the heel of the shoe and slid off with it.

Amy stared at her foot—or she would have, if she could have seen it. Her entire left foot was invisible!

Amy panicked. She pulled up the leg of her jeans. Her left leg was there, all right, but her left foot had completely vanished.

"Eeeeeeek!" Amy shrieked. She couldn't help it. Her missing foot was too creepy.

The room grew silent, and the girls turned to stare at her. Amy quickly slipped her sock back on so no one would see her problem. Then Ms. Lawrence, the gym teacher, rushed in.

"What's going on in here?" she asked.

"It's Amy," Keesha said. "I think she's hurt."

"I'm all right!" Amy said quickly. "I just—I bumped my head on my locker."

"Better get to the nurse's office, then," Ms. Lawrence snapped.

Amy gratefully put her shoe back on and left the locker room. Her face blushed red as she felt the other girls staring at her. The school nurse saw how flustered she looked and told her to lie down on the cot for a few minutes.

Thoughts raced through Amy's mind as she stared up at the ceiling. The necklace had been in her pocket the whole time, she was sure of that. So why was her foot invisible? Was it permanent?

Then Amy heard a familiar voice in the front

office. It was Keesha.

"I just want to check on Amy," Keesha was telling the nurse.

Amy panicked. She couldn't talk to Keesha now—not with an invisible foot. Amy touched the necklace in her pocket. There was one way she could avoid Keesha—but was it really safe? Amy wasn't so sure anymore.

If Amy uses the necklace to avoid Keesha, go to page 74.

If Amy talks to Keesha, go to page 119.

Continued from page 79

When I stomped on the stone, I broke it, Amy thought. *But I didn't destroy it. Maybe if I destroy the stone, I'll destroy the Shadow People.*

Amy found her courage. She scooped up the necklace and dashed across her room to her bookshelf. The Shadow People felt like ice against her skin as she brushed past them. Amy grabbed a heavy bookend shaped like a monkey. She put the necklace on the floor and smashed it hard with the monkey. Then she smashed it again, and again, and again.

Amy had crushed the stone into a fine power.

"That's got to work," she muttered.

But the Shadow People didn't vanish. They formed another circle around Amy, and began to swirl around and around. Amy felt her body grow lighter and lighter. Her feet lifted off of the floor, and one of the Shadow People grabbed her hand. They swirled faster and faster. When Amy looked down at her body, she saw that she had become transparent from head to toe. Then the shadow people began to chant.

"You are one of us now, Amy!"

THE END

Billy agreed that it couldn't hurt to check the library first. Amy and he came up with a plan: Amy would bring the necklace to school with her the next day. After school, Amy would go to the library and if the coast was clear, Billy would materialize.

"It's hard to explain, but I can kind of materialize a little when the necklace is near," Billy said. "Not so that anyone can see me, but so I can see and hear what's going on."

Amy liked the idea that Billy would be close by. It was like having a secret friend.

During school the next day, Billy made her laugh by whispering jokes in her ear during class. When lunchtime came, Amy sat alone at her usual table. She wished Billy could materialize and eat with her, but it was too risky.

Amy was whispering to Billy and eating her peanut-butter sandwich when a fist pounded the table in front of her. Amy looked up to see David Pierson leaning over the table with a wicked grin on his face.

"Look, she's talking to herself!" David shouted, loud enough for everyone in the lunchroom to hear. "It's crazy Amy!"

Amy's cheeks burned red. She wanted to crawl under the table.

David reached out and grabbed her lunch bag. He stuck his hand inside and pulled out a plastic bag filled with homemade cookies.

"Mmmm, cookies," he said. "Thanks, crazy Amy!"

Amy sat, helpless, as David took a huge bite of cookie. Tears stung her eyes, and she ran out of the lunchroom into the schoolyard.

Billy appeared next to her.

"That boy is a no-good fink," Billy said. "You should stand up to him."

"What am I supposed to do?" Amy said, sniffling. "I can't fight him."

"No, but you can turn invisible," Billy said, his eyes shining. "Come on, Amy, think of what fun we could have. Let's get even with that rat before we go to the library! I'll help you."

Amy wasn't sure what to say. She would love to get even with David Pierson. But it just seemed hopeless.

If Amy refuses Billy's help, go to page 80.

If Amy accepts Billy's help, go to page 89.

Continued from page 110

"I can't steal the test answers," Amy said. "It's just not right."

"Yeah," Keesha said. "I agree with Amy."

Amy smiled at Keesha. She should have known that her old friend would stick by her.

Shelby grimaced. "You guys are no fun," she said. "Can you let me try on the necklace now? I haven't had a turn yet."

Amy hesitated. She didn't know Shelby that well. Could she trust her with the necklace?

"Come on, Amy," Shelby whined. "Don't be rude."

Amy sighed and handed Shelby the necklace. Shelby clasped it around her neck.

Nothing happened.

"Hey!" she yelled. "How come I'm not invisible?"

"I don't know," Amy said. "It worked for me and Keesha."

Amy looked at her friend, but Keesha's face had grown pale. She was pointing at Shelby, her mouth open in shock.

Amy followed Amy's gaze. Blue hairs were sprouting up on Shelby's face and arms. Her eyebrows looked like bushy blue caterpillars. And that wasn't all. Small, white horns sprouted from Shelby's forehead.

Shelby noticed the girls and looked down at her arms.

"What's happening?" she shrieked.

"You're turning into some kind of monster," Amy said. "Take the necklace off—quick!"

Shelby tore the necklace off of her neck. Then she threw it to the ground and stepped on it with her shoe.

"What are you doing?" Amy yelled. She bent down to grab the necklace, but Shelby had destroyed it.

The horns and blue fur were slowly disappearing from Shelby's body, but she still looked furious.

"What kind of trick was that, Amy?" Shelby wailed. "Keesha and I are never going to speak to you again—right, Keesha?"

Keesha put an arm around Amy.

"Forget it, Shelby," she said. "I'll talk to Amy if I want to. Amy didn't do anything wrong. I bet that necklace turned you into a monster because you act like one!"

Amy followed Keesha as she walked out of the clubhouse. She tried to sort out everything that had happened.

Her necklace was destroyed. She'd never be

able to turn invisible again.

But Keesha was her friend again. That felt pretty good. Better than being invisible, even.

"Hey, Keesha," Amy said, "can I eat lunch with you tomorrow?"

THE END

Continued from page 46

Amy was curious to see what might be in the museum. She and Billy made plans to go there the next day after school. Amy would tell her mom that she had to do research for a school project.

That night, Amy slept with the necklace next to her pillow. Billy decided to go back to the Shadow World for the night.

"I can't explain it exactly," he said. "But it takes extra energy for me to appear in the real world. I could use a rest, anyway."

After school the next day, Amy ran all the way home. She found Billy in her room, examining the necklace.

"Let's go," Amy said. "The museum closes at six today."

Billy nodded. "Take the necklace with you. I'll keep out of sight until we get there."

Amy's mom dropped her off at the museum. She waved goodbye and then climbed up the white marble steps. Amy had been there more times than she could count. Her dad especially loved to wander through the musty rooms.

Most of the exhibits focused on the history of Bleaktown, starting with the Native Americans who first inhabited the area. There were displays of old-fashioned clothing, and pictures of how Main Street looked one hundred years ago, and even cases filled with dead butterflies pinned on paper. Amy had no idea where to look for the symbols on the necklace. She slipped behind a tall, potted plant and took the necklace out of its box.

"Billy," she whispered, "are you there?"

Billy appeared next to her.

"Where do we go?" she asked.

"The thing I saw was part of some old lady's art collection," Billy said. "Do you know where that is?"

Amy did. It was her father's favorite exhibit. Agatha Bleaker-Higgins was a member of one of Bleaktown's wealthiest families. She spent many years traveling the world, collecting strange paintings and sculptures. When she died, she left many pieces in her collection to the museum.

Amy closed the lid to the box, and Billy disappeared again. Then Amy hurried to the display.

The museum was a maze of twists and turns, and Amy made several until she reached the dimlylit collection of Agatha Bleaker-Higgins. The hallway was empty, so Amy told Billy it was safe to materialize.

"Here we are," Amy said. "Do you see it?"

Amy watched as Billy scanned the display. The small area had been set up as a replica of Agatha's sitting room from the 1900s. Behind a red velvet rope sat Agatha's huge mahogany desk and her red velvet chair. Paintings hung on the walls, and sturdy bookshelves held an array of sculptures and other strange items.

Suddenly, Billy pointed to the desk.

"There it is!" he cried. "See the symbols?"

Amy leaned over the rope. On top of the desk, nestled among an inkwell and a pile of books, was some kind of paperweight. It looked like a small cube made of silver. As Amy leaned closer, she could see designs carved into the silver.

Billy was right. They were just like the symbols on the necklace.

"That's amazing," Amy said. "What do we do now?"

Billy looked from left to right.

"No one's here," he said. "Let's take it home and see what it's about."

"You mean steal it?" Amy asked.

"More like borrowing," Billy said. "We can bring it back when we're done. Let's do it fast. Someone could come by any second!"

If Amy refuses to "borrow" the cube, go to page 22.
If Amy agrees to "borrow" the cube, go to page 132.

Continued from page 64

It couldn't hurt to put the necklace back on for a few minutes, Amy reasoned. She just couldn't face Keesha right now.

Amy quickly put the necklace around her neck. A second later, Keesha and the nurse walked into the room.

"That's funny," the nurse said. "I sent Amy in here to lie down just a few minutes ago. She must have gone back to gym when I was looking in my files."

"I didn't see her there," Keesha said. "I'd better go check."

Amy realized she'd have to leave the room and become visible again somewhere else. There were so many things to think about when you were invisible!

Amy walked out of the office behind Keesha. Then she ran down the hall back to the gym as fast as she could. By the time Keesha got there, Amy was visible again.

"I looked in the nurse's office for you," Keesha said. "I was worried."

"Thanks," Amy said. "I'm fine."

Somehow it was nice to know that Keesha was worried about her. Amy vowed not to use the necklace again in school. And she avoided looking at her invisible foot.

Maybe it's just a side effect or something, she thought. *I'm sure it'll be back to normal when I get home.*

But when Amy got home, she found that her left foot was still invisible. And that wasn't all. The invisibility had spread up her leg, to right under her knee. Amy's right foot and lower leg had vanished, too.

Amy felt like crying. It was fun using the necklace to turn invisible, but this was something else. For all she knew, the invisibility would keep creeping up and up until her whole body was invisible—forever.

And the necklace was responsible for all of it. Amy wished her Aunt Irene had never given it to her.

Then Amy remembered something. Aunt Irene said she had bought the necklace from a shop in town. Maybe the store owner might be able to tell Amy more about the necklace—and help her with her problem.

Go to page 84.

Continued from page 113.

Amy wasn't sure if she should do it, but she really wanted to help Billy. She put the necklace around her neck to give the magic an extra boost. Then she stepped inside.

Immediately, a strange sound filled her ears, like the sound you hear when you hold a conch shell to your ear, only louder. The room vanished, and to Amy it seemed that she and Billy were standing in a large room, a room with no walls or ceiling. Gray mist swirled around them.

"Where are we?" Amy asked.

"This is the Shadow World," Billy said. "At least that's what I call it. See?"

Billy pointed to their feet. Below the swirling mist, Amy could see her bedroom. There was her bed, and the circle she had drawn, but Amy and Billy were not there. Her room looked so close, but when Amy reached down to touch it, the vision disappeared.

Amy's heart began to beat faster. "Maybe I shouldn't have stepped into the circle with you," she said.

"Maybe it's the necklace," Billy said. "Take it off and see what happens."

Amy unclasped the necklace and put it in her

pocket, but nothing changed.

"This is terrible!" Amy wailed. "How do we get out?"

Billy chewed on his bottom lip while he thought. "Hey," he said finally, "that book said there was a crown, a necklace, and a coin, right? All we have to do is wait for somebody to find the crown, and then maybe we can communicate with them, like I did with you."

Amy brightened. "That could work," she said. Then fear gripped her again. "Billy, how long did you wait before I got the necklace?"

Billy shrugged. "I'm not sure," he said. "When I came here, it was 1952."

"That means . . ." Amy's voice trailed off as she felt her last shred of hope fade away. " . . . you've been trapped here for more than fifty years!"

THE END

Continued from page 55

Amy had had enough of the necklace. She tore the chain from her neck, not even bothering to undo the clasp. Then she threw it to the ground and stomped on it hard with her foot.

Amy lifted up her foot and saw that the stone was broken into three pieces. Thin tendrils of white smoke swirled out of the stones. The smoke swirled upward, growing thicker and larger with each second. Soon the room was filled with white. Amy felt like she was standing in the middle of a fog.

Uh oh, Amy thought. *This can't be good.*

As the white fog began to settle, Amy saw that it was taking shape—human shape. Soon a crowd of transparent people filled her room. Amy saw an old man in a hat; a tall, thin, teenage girl; a boy in a baseball uniform—there were too many to keep track of. They were filmy, just like Adam, and they all wore sad expressions. Their eyes looked dull and blank.

Amy found she was frozen with fear. These ghostly people didn't look friendly, that was for sure. But she couldn't run or scream.

Then they all began to speak, their mouths moving in unison.

"We are the Shadow People," they said, in one voice that sounded like a cold wind. "You can be one of us now, Amy."

The Shadow People began to circle Amy, getting closer and closer. Amy closed her eyes and tried to think.

The people had appeared when she broke the white stone. To get rid of them, she probably had to do something else to the necklace. But what should she do?

If Amy glues the stone back together, go to page 12.

**If Amy decides to crush the stone into tiny pieces,
go to page 65.**

"It's no use, Billy," Amy said. "Just forget about it, okay?"

Billy shrugged and disappeared again. Amy didn't see him again until after school, when she went to the library. As she had predicted, no one else was there.

"We've got the place to ourselves," Amy said. "Let's start looking."

Amy and Billy searched for about a half hour and found some good possibilities. There was a book of ancient languages, a book of museum treasures, and one on the history of magic.

Amy carried the books in her arms as she hurried home.

"Something tells me the answer is in here somewhere," she whispered to Billy as she walked. "We're going to get you out of the Shadow World—I promise."

"Hey, look! Crazy Amy's talking to herself again!"

David Pierson ran across the street and jumped right in front of her, grinning that same wicked grin.

"Need help with your books?" he asked, and in the next instant, he knocked them from her arms.

"Cut it out," Amy protested weakly. She bent down to pick up the books--and the necklace slipped out of her pocket. She tried to grab it, but David beat her to it.

"Oooh, how pretty," David teased. "I'd bet you'd like it back, wouldn't you?"

"Give it!" Amy shouted. David couldn't take her necklace—he just couldn't.

David swung the necklace around his head.

"Sorry, crazy Amy," he said. "It's mine now!"

The necklace flew out of David's hands and fell through the sewer grate. Amy rushed to the grate, bending down, but there was nothing to see but blackness. She heard the sound of rushing water as the sewer carried the necklace away forever.

"No!" Amy screamed. "You big jerk! Look what you have done!"

But David was already halfway down the street, laughing.

Amy sank to the ground, crushed. The necklace was gone. Billy was gone forever. She couldn't help him now.

"I should have listened to Billy," Amy moaned. "None of this would have happened if I had stood up to David."

THE END

Continued from page 103

Amy wanted to scream, to cry out loud, but she couldn't--not in front of everyone in the lunchroom. Instead, she stood up, pushing Adam away with her. Then she ran through the back door into the empty schoolyard.

Deep in her heart, Amy knew it was no use. She couldn't keep running forever. Adam and the Shadow People would just keep coming for her . . . and coming. She couldn't escape them.

Frustrated and exhausted, Amy fell to her knees in the grass. She felt a cold touch on her neck, then heard a tiny click.

Adam had attached the necklace around her neck.

Amy stood up and spun around.

"No!" she cried. "I won't go with you. I'm not one of you. I'm not!"

The Shadow People crowded around her now.

"It's too late, Amy," Adam said. "Just look at yourself."

Amy looked down. To her horror, she saw that her body was transparent, just like the others.

Like a picture on a movie screen, she thought, a cold calm sweeping over her. That's just what she thought when she had first seen Adam.

Amy quickly flushed with anger.

"No," she said. "I'm not one of you. I'll prove it."

Amy ran across the grass and burst into the lunchroom.

"Hey everybody!" she yelled. "It's Amy! Over here!"

But not a single person looked her way.

"Over here!" Amy screamed, as loudly as she could.

Adam put a hand on her shoulder. For the first time, it didn't feel cold.

"It's no use, Amy," he said. "You should have screamed before, when someone might have heard you. But it's too late now."

"Noooo!" Amy screamed, but in her heart, she knew Adam was right. It was too late.

She was one of the Shadow People now.

THE END

Continued from page 75

Amy searched the necklace's black box. On the bottom she saw a tiny gold label that she hadn't noticed before. It read:

Sebastian Cream's
JunkShop

Amy found a map of Bleaktown in the phone book and looked up the street. Then, with a twinge of guilt, Amy told her mom she was going to the library to study. It wasn't exactly a lie, she thought. Wary Lane was on the way to the library, at least.

In a few minutes, Amy was walking down Wary Lane. Tall, leafy trees lined the street, blocking out the sun. When she reached number 5, she stopped and stared.

The front window of Sebastian Cream's Junk Shop was like nothing she had ever seen before. Every inch of the display area was crammed with strange and unusual objects . . . a marble statue of a Greek goddess . . . a pink carousel horse with peeling paint . . . a red velvet cape that looked like it had been worn by a king.

Amy could have stared at the window for hours, but she remembered her invisible legs and snapped out of her trance. She opened the door and stepped inside.

The rest of the store was just as packed as the display window. Among the clutter, Amy saw a short man polishing blue-glass bottles that were stacked on a shelf. He turned when he saw Amy.

"Sebastian Cream," he said, giving a little bow. "May I help you?"

For a second, Amy thought about turning around and running out of the store. She didn't know what to say. *My aunt gave me a necklace from your store and now my legs are half invisible? He would probably call the police.*

"Uh, n-no thanks," Amy muttered.

Mr. Cream pushed his wire-rimmed glasses down on his nose and stared at Amy for a few seconds.

"You must be Irene's niece," he said finally. "Charming lady. Are you enjoying the necklace?"

Amy wasn't sure what to say. How did Mr. Cream know who she was? At any other time, she might have been scared, but there something about the little man put her at ease. With the ring of white hair on his head and his bright green eyes, he looked almost like some kind of elf.

Amy took a deep breath. "I need to know

about the necklace," she said carefully. "It's very
. . . unusual."

Amy handed Mr. Cream the box, and he
snapped open the lid.

"This is a very unusual piece indeed," he said.
He shuffled over to the shop's counter and disappeared behind it. When he emerged, he was holding a thick old book with a cracked leather cover.
He began to flip through the pages. Finally, he
stopped, and beckoned for Amy to come closer.

"It's coming back to me," he said. "The woman
who sold me this necklace claimed it had a
strange power. She wanted to get rid of it very
badly."

Amy's heart began to beat fast. "She did? What
else did she say?"

Mr. Cream closed the book.

"Nothing," he said. "Anything else?"

"Yes!" Amy cried. "I mean, I need to know
more. Please. I have a . . . a problem."

Amy lifted the leg of her jeans. Mr. Cream did
not seem shocked at all to see that Amy's leg was
missing. He thoughtfully rubbed his chin.

"Very interesting," he said.

Interesting? Amy felt like screaming. There
was nothing interesting about having invisible
legs. It was terrifying.

Mr. Cream leaned forward and looked directly

at Amy.

"The answers to your questions are already inside you," he said. "You have more to learn from the necklace."

What did that mean? Amy thought his answer sounded more like a riddle.

"But my legs!" Amy protested.

"I'm sure they'll be fine," Mr. Cream. "At least, I think they will."

The little man pressed the necklace into Amy's hands and pushed her toward the door.

"I'll be seeing you!" he said cheerfully.

Maybe not, Amy thought, as she shuffled out of the store. *Maybe soon no one will be able to see me.*

The thought haunted Amy all through supper. When she changed into her pajamas, she saw that now she was invisible all the way up to her belly button.

Amy stifled a scream. She took out the necklace and stared at the strange symbols as her invisible legs dangled over the bed. There had to be an answer there somewhere. Someway to turn things back to normal . . .

Amy drifted off to sleep, still clutching the necklace. The symbols danced through her dreams. Then a sudden blast of freezing air woke her up.

"Hello, Amy."

It was Adam. And he was surrounded by others like him—see-through people who crowded around her bed.

If Amy confronts Adam and the see-through people, go to page 99.

If Amy runs away, go to page 121.

Continued from page 67

"You have a point," Amy said. "I can turn invisible, after all. I should be able to do something good with it."

Billy smiled. "That's the spirit."

After school, Amy followed David and his friends outside. They usually hung out in front of the school, goofing around and hassling people as they tried to go home. Amy hid behind a tree and watched them.

"What should I do?" she asked Billy.

"Well, first you should turn invisible," he said.

Amy put on the necklace. As soon as she turned invisible, she noticed that Billy seemed more solid than before.

"Cool," Amy said. "I wonder if I become part of the Shadow World when I'm invisible? Maybe that's why I can see you better here."

"Maybe," Billy said. "We can figure that out later. Now, let's have some fun."

Amy walked over to where David and his friends were hanging out. They were talking about some video game they all played.

"And then I went pow! And, like, the monster's guts went flying!" David was saying. One of his friends gave him a high-five.

"This is going to be fun," Billy said. "Now, here's what you should do."

Billy whispered instructions in Amy's ear. They sounded kind of mean to her, but somehow, being invisible made doing them easier.

First she tied David's shoelaces together. Then she picked up his backpack, opened it up, and dumped his books and papers out onto the ground.

"Hey, who did that?" David asked, jumping up. "That's not funny, guys!"

David tried to step forward, but instead he fell flat on his face into the grass. His friends burst out laughing.

"That's pretty funny, dude!" one of them said.

"Whatever," David said, scowling. He untied his shoelaces. Then he stuffed his papers back into his backpack. "I'm going home."

David stomped off, and Amy felt strangely satisfied—and just a little guilty.

"That was great!" Billy said as they walked back to the tree.

"It did feel pretty good," Amy admitted, taking off the necklace. "Now let's check out the library!"

The library turned out to be a good idea. Amy left with an armful of books about ancient treasures, museum exhibits, and even a history of magic.

Mrs. Izzo raised an eyebrow when Amy walked through the door.

"Book report," Amy explained.

"It's nice to see you're so prepared," her mom replied. "Would you mind starting a little later? I need you to watch Mikey while I cook dinner."

By the time Amy and Billy cracked open the books, it was already dark. Amy had scanned through *The Treasures of Ancient Egypt* and had just started on *The History of Magic* when she felt her eyelids droop. Amy yawned.

"Don't you get tired in the Shadow World?" she asked Billy.

"Not really," Billy said. "You can go to sleep if you want. I can keep looking."

Billy's offer was tempting. Amy was really tired. But she was also anxious to find out more about her necklace.

If Amy stays awake until she and Billy find an answer, go to page 111.

If Amy goes to sleep, go to page 139.

Continued from page 131

The room was stark white and practically empty except for a glass case in the center of the room. Amy and James walked to the case, and Amy shone her flashlight on it.

Inside the case were three talismans. They looked like Amy's necklace, but one talisman had a red stone in the center, and the other had a black stone. Amy took the necklace out of her pocket and held it up next to the two talismans. It looked like the missing piece of a set.

Besides the talismans, the case also held a small book, crumbling with age.

"The Secret to the Talismans of Power," Amy read aloud.

"These must be the original talismans!" James said, his voice rising. "Two of them, anyway."

"You are correct."

Amy's blood ran cold. The voice belonged to Diamanda. She stood in the doorway, flanked by two men dressed in gray.

"We have been searching for the original Invisibility talisman for years," Diamanda said, eyeing Amy's necklace. "And now you have brought it to us. How kind of you."

"We're not here to help you," James snapped.

"We're here to find my uncle!"

Diamanda laughed. "So Marshall sent you here. Very well. You shall join him."

Diamanda snapped her fingers and the two men rushed forward. There was nowhere to run.

"Amy, use the necklace!" James hissed in her ear. "You can escape!"

Amy pulled the necklace out of her pocket. Turning invisible might be her only chance to get away. But could she leave James at the mercy of the Shadow Society?

If Amy uses the necklace to become invisible, go to page 104.

If Amy decides to stick with James, go to page 141.

Continued from page 16

"What could it hurt to knock on the door?"
Amy said out loud, finding her courage. "People
knock on doors all the time. And probably no
one's there anyway."

Amy crossed the street and climbed the steps.
To the left of the door was a round black button.
Amy pressed the button and waited. She nervous-
ly fumbled with the necklace chain in her hands.

Soon Amy heard footsteps, and the door slowly
opened. A tall woman wearing a long, gray dress
opened the door.

"Yes?" she asked. Her voice sounded cold and
serious.

"I, uh," Amy wasn't sure how to begin.

Then the woman noticed the necklace in
Amy's hands, and her eyes brightened.

"Oh, please come in," she said. "I didn't realize
you belonged. You must be our youngest member
yet."

Amy had no idea what the woman was talking
about, but she was more curious than ever now.
She stepped through the doorway and followed
the woman into a long, dark hall.

The woman walked swiftly down the corridor.

"The meeting is about to start," she said.

"You're just in time."

"Meeting?" Amy asked. "I'm not sure I—"

The woman stopped and turned around. "Don't be nervous. This is a wonderful thing we're doing. You should be proud to be part of it." Then she opened a door and motioned for Amy to step inside.

Amy gasped. They had entered a large, round room that looked like an auditorium. Rows of seats circled a small round stage in the room's center. Most of the seats were filled with people dressed in gray. Amy thought she recognized some people from her neighborhood. In the front row was a boy who looked a lot like the boy who had appeared to Amy in front of the school.

A tall woman stood on the stage next to a small table. She wore a long gray robe with a hood. She had light blond hair and a face that would have been pretty, Amy thought, if there wasn't something slightly sinister about it. She had cold blue eyes and an even colder smile.

Amy suddenly felt uncomfortable. She turned toward the door, but the woman who had let her in pushed her into a nearby seat. Amy sat, unsure of what to do next.

You wanted to find out more about the necklace, a little voice inside of her said. *It looks like you came to the right place.*

Amy tried to relax. It was just a meeting, after all. When it was over, she could leave.

Then the blond woman on stage raised her arms in the air, and the low chatter in the room went silent.

"Welcome, members of the Bleaktown Shadow Society," she said.

Everyone applauded. Amy gave a few weak claps so she wouldn't look out of place.

"Hooray for Diamanda!" someone cried out. The woman on the stage nodded, and Amy guessed that must be her name.

"The time of our great mission is drawing near," Diamanda said. "Soon we will see our magnificent plan come to fruition."

Diamanda picked up what looked like a remote control from the table and pressed a button. Instantly, three holographic images floated in the air in front of her. Amy tried to hide her surprise. There were three circles, each with different symbols. One of the circles looked just like her necklace!

"These ancient talismans were created to give special abilities to the bearer," Diamanda said. "One for transportation, one for invisibility, and one for ultimate power."

So that was it! Amy thought. She knew there was something special about her necklace.

"The Shadow Society has worked for centuries to create copies of the talismans that each of you hold. They are very powerful," Diamanda continued. "And with that power, we will achieve our goal!"

Amy sat on the edge of her seat. What exactly was this great plan, anyway?

"Together we will transport Bleaktown to the shadow dimension!" Diamanda cried. "We will save Bleaktown from the evils of modern society!

The crowd burst into applause. Amy sank back into her seat, astounded. Transport Bleaktown into the shadow dimension? That didn't sound good at all. She scanned the room, looking for a way out.

"And now we will proceed to the roof," Diamanda said. "It is time."

Everyone rose to their seats, and Amy found herself being pushed along with the crowd. They walked around the edge of the circular room. Thick white columns rose to the ceiling against the back wall.

Panicked, Amy looked for an exit. Then she heard a voice hiss her name.

"Amy!"

Amy stopped. The voice was coming from behind one of the columns. Amy broke away and stepped toward the voice.

Amy saw the figure of a boy hiding behind the pillar.

"Follow me!" whispered the boy.

Amy paused. Was this the way out she was looking for—or would it lead to more trouble?

If Amy follows the boy, go to page 38.

If Amy goes along with the others, go to page 47.

Continued from page 88

Amy's first instinct was to run away. But she stopped herself. If she wanted answers, she'd have to be brave.

Amy found her voice. "Who are you?" she asked. "What do you want with me?"

Adam stepped forward from the group.

"We're just like you, Amy," he said. "We were all shy once. But then we found the magic. The magic to set us free."

"What do you mean?" Amy asked. "What kind of magic?"

Adam clasped the lucky coin he wore around his neck.

"The magic of the symbols," he said.

Amy looked at the group of shadowy people. They were all different--an old man in a hat; a tall, thin teenage girl; a boy in a baseball uniform. But they all had one thing in common. They each wore a necklace, or medallion, or a lucky coin like Adam's. And they all were engraved with the same strange symbols.

"My necklace has those symbols, too," Amy said, feeling a little braver. "It can make me turn invisible. But now I'm starting to turn invisible for good. I'm scared."

"Don't be scared," Adam said. "It's much better here."

"What do you mean, 'here'?" Amy asked, confused.

Adam smiled, but it wasn't exactly a happy smile. "We live in the Shadow World," he said. "No one can bother you in the Shadow World. You don't have to talk to people. You don't have to make friends. It's the perfect place."

The other Shadow People slowly nodded their heads.

"What if I don't want to go to the Shadow World?" Amy asked.

Adam laughed, and it sounded like icy rain falling.

"You'll be one of us soon," he said. "Just keep wearing the necklace."

Then he and the Shadow People faded from her sight.

Amy rubbed her eyes. Had it all been a dream? But her skin still shivered from the cold feeling that the Shadow People gave off. It had been real. All of it.

Amy crawled back under the covers. She had gone to sleep searching for answers about the necklace and its powers, and now she had some answers. She thought about what Adam had said. He hadn't really told her anything helpful—or

had he? Adam said if she kept wearing the necklace, she would become one of the Shadow
People. Maybe if she *stopped* wearing the necklace,
she could become totally visible again.

That has to be it, Amy thought. *All I have to do is
stop wearing the necklace, and everything will go back to
normal.*

But, another thought crept into Amy's mind.

Who wants to go back to normal? a little voice
teased her. *When things were normal, you had no
friends. You didn't know how to talk to anybody. Maybe
Adam is right. Maybe the Shadow World is the perfect
place. . .*

Amy drifted off to sleep. In her dreams, she
saw herself walking through the school hallways,
silent and alone, as groups of laughing and talking kids walked right past her. She opened the
door to the girls' bathroom, entered, walked up to
the mirror . . . and saw nothing.

Amy woke with a start. Morning sunlight
streamed through the window. Panicked, Amy ran
to her dresser and looked in the mirror.

Her own tired face stared back at her.
Relieved, Amy checked to see that her invisibility
hadn't spread any further. Things hadn't gotten
any better—but they hadn't gotten any worse,
either.

Amy wore long jeans and high socks to cover

any trace of her mysterious ailment. She thought about leaving the necklace at home, but at the last second decided to take it.

"I won't wear it," she promised herself. "I'll just keep it safe."

The rest of the morning started like any other day. Amy managed to avoid talking to Keesha, and at lunchtime, she found a quiet table all to herself in a corner.

It's not like I'm avoiding anybody, she reasoned. *I just need to work out this necklace thing by myself.*

Amy dug her spoon into the container of strawberry yogurt her mom had packed her, when she felt a cold chill. Looking up, she saw that Adam and the Shadow People had surrounded her table. She gasped.

"Why haven't you put on the necklace, Amy?" Adam asked. This time, he wasn't smiling. "We're waiting for you."

"M-m-maybe I don't want to go the Shadow World," she said. "Maybe I like it here."

Adam snorted. "Look around you, Amy. Nobody here likes you. You'll be better off with us."

Adam reached into Amy's pocket and took out the little black box. Then he opened the lid and took out the necklace, dangling it in front of her face.

"Put it on, Amy," he said. "You're one of us now."

Amy felt frozen with fear, unable to move. None of the kids in the lunchroom even seemed to noticed what was happening. They probably couldn't see Adam and the others, and they never paid attention to Amy, anyway.

Adam draped the chain around Amy's neck and started to fasten the clasp. If Amy didn't do something, she'd wind up in the Shadow World forever.

If Amy runs from the shadow people, go to page 82.

If Amy screams for help, go to page 116.

"Amy, do it!" James hissed. "It's no good if we both get caught."

James had a point, but Amy still felt a pang of guilt as she slipped on the necklace. She saw the look of surprise on Diamanda's face when she turned invisible.

Amy rushed forward, running past Diamanda and the two guards. As she tore off down the hall, she heard James cry out behind her. She also heard Diamanda yell something about a trapdoor.

It didn't matter. Amy just had to find the exit.

Suddenly, Amy felt her feet fly out from underneath her. The fall sent her body sliding down some kind of metal chute.

Then she was falling through air. She braced herself and landed on a hard floor with a thud.

Amy slowly sat up. She was sore, but not badly hurt. To her surprise, she saw a black-haired man standing over her. Amy recognized his face.

"You're James's uncle," she said. "But what happened?"

"This house is full of booby-traps," Uncle Marshall told her. "You must have slipped through a trapdoor."

Amy scanned the room. It looked like a prison

cell. A wood bench leaned against one of the stone gray walls. The only light came from a single bulb swinging from the high ceiling.

"Is there a way out of here?" Amy asked.

Uncle Marshall shook his head. "I've tried. The trapdoor chute is completely vertical. It's impossible to climb up."

Amy felt a sick feeling in her stomach. "So you mean . . ."

"We're trapped," Uncle Marshall said. "The Shadow Society has won."

THE END

Nothing, Amy told herself grimly. *There's nothing you can do. You can't even make friends at school. How are you supposed to save Bleaktown?*

Diamanda began to chant words from the book. They didn't sound like any language Amy had ever heard before.

The other members of the society chanted along with Diamanda. At first, nothing happened.

But then the stones in the talismans began to glow.

"It's happening!" Diamanda murmured, her eyes gleaming.

A small gray cloud appeared in the center of the circle. Amy watched, transfixed, as the cloud grew larger and began to take shape. Its body sprouted two long arms with skeletal fingers. A huge, shapeless head grazed the top of the ceiling. The monster—for that's definitely what it had to be—had two dark, dark eyes and a wide, gaping mouth.

"Is this supposed to happen?" the old man asked, confused.

"I-I'm not sure," Diamanda stammered. She cleared her throat. "Oh great one! Will you lead our town into the Shadow World?"

The monster didn't answer. Its body began to grow and expand some more. Its head crashed through the ceiling. Its arms smashed through the walls of the room.

Amy and the others ran from the room, dodging falling plaster. Once outside, they could see that the monster was growing and growing. Soon it would block out the sky.

Amy ran to Diamanda. She had finally found the courage to speak out.

"This is your fault!" Amy cried. "This monster is going to destroy our town! Can't you stop it?"

"I don't know how!" Diamanda wailed.

Amy screamed with frustration. There was nothing she could do. Nothing except run home and warn her family. Maybe they could leave before it was too late.

A few minutes later, Amy ran into her living room, breathless. Her mom and Mikey were playing with blocks on the floor.

"Mom, listen to me!" Amy said. "It's important! We've got to—"

"Oh there you are, Amy," Mrs. Izzo said. "I'm glad you're home."

Amy heard the thunderous footsteps of the monster getting closer and closer.

"You've got to listen to me, Mom—"

Mrs. Izzo interrupted her again. "Not now,

Amy. It's about time you sat down and wrote a thank-you note to Aunt Irene for that lovely necklace she gave you."

THE END

Continued from page 44

Amy reluctantly agreed to show the necklace to Shelby. It felt good to be friends with Keesha again, and she didn't want to lose her.

Keesha arranged a meeting at Shelby's house the next day after school. Shelby had a clubhouse in her backyard that her parents had specially made.

"So what's this big secret you guys have?" Shelby asked.

Amy and Shelby looked a little bit alike, except that Shelby just always looked a little more perfect. Shelby's brown hair was waist-long and thick, and her brown eyes were flecked with bits of gold.

"Amy's got this amazing necklace," Keesha said. "Show her, Amy."

Amy took out the necklace and demonstrated its powers. Keesha used the necklace to turn invisible, too. When they were done, Shelby's mind was whirling a hundred miles a minute.

"Think of all the things we could do with this!" she said. "For starters, there's that math test on Friday. Everyone knows Mr. Moore's tests are so unfair. We could use the necklace to turn invisible and steal the answers!"

Amy frowned. Stealing test answers was cheating, plain and simple. She didn't want to do it. But she didn't want to stop being friends with Keesha, either.

If Amy agrees to steal the test answers, go to page 28.

If Amy refuses to steal the test answers, go to page 68.

Continued from page 91

Amy forced herself to stay awake.

"I'm not going to sleep now," she said. "We're close to an answer. I can feel it somehow."

Amy scanned the pages of *The History of Magic* until her eyes got blurry. Then something made her stop.

It was a black-and-white photograph of an ancient scroll. Written on the crackled paper were symbols—the same symbols on Amy's necklace.

"I found something!" Amy said excitedly. Billy looked over her shoulder as she read on.

According to the book, the scroll had been discovered hundreds of years ago by three explorers in the Middle East. The explorers brought the scroll back to Europe to try to decipher the language, but one by one, they had disappeared.

The scroll was locked away in a museum, but rumors soon spread that a sorcerer named Archimedes Grim had copied down the symbols first. Amy shivered when she saw a photo of Grim. The man had a thin, pinched face, a black mustache that curled at the ends, and eyes that seemed to be staring at Amy from the page. He definitely looked like some kind of sorcerer.

Amy forced herself to look away from the

photo and kept reading. The book said that Archimedes Grim had used the symbols to create three objects of power—a crown, a necklace, and a coin.

"This is it!" Amy cried. "You must have found the coin. And I found the necklace."

"It makes sense," Billy said. "But how does that help me get out of the Shadow World?"

Amy kept reading. "It says here that Grim found that the symbols had their greatest power when they were arranged in a circle. Someone said they saw him draw the circles on the ground. When he stepped inside the circle, he disappeared."

Billy looked thoughtful. "Maybe that magic would work for me, too," Billy said. "We could draw the symbols in a circle, just like the sorcerer did. If I step inside it, I might disappear from the Shadow World and appear in this world."

Amy felt wide awake now. It was definitely worth a try.

First, she crept into Mikey's room. Her little brother had one of those big easels with giant rolls of paper so he could color without making a mess. Amy tore off a large piece of paper and snuck back into her room. Then she used the necklace as a model and drew the symbols on the paper with a marker.

Billy took a deep breath. "Here goes."

He stepped into the circle, but nothing happened.

Billy frowned. "Rats!" he said. Then he had an idea. "Amy, maybe you should stand in the circle with me. The power of the necklace might be just what we need to make this work."

It made sense, Amy knew. Still, the idea of stepping into the circle made her nervous. What if something went wrong?

If Amy steps into the circle, go to page 76.

If Amy refuses to step into the circle, go to page 134.

"Wait a second," Amy said. "You brought all that stuff in your backpack. Do you have a compass?"

James slapped his forehead.

"Of course!" he said. "Uncle Marshall told me to always carry one."

James ran into the shed, where he had left his backpack. He came out a few moments later with a compass.

Amy and James watched as the compass found north. They followed the line that pointed east—in the opposite direction of the Bleaktown Bank.

"I guess you were right," James admitted. "Now we know where east is. Let's do this thing!"

Amy brought out the talismans from the shed while James followed the directions in the book to draw a circle in the dirt. They placed the talismans on the ground inside the circle. Then James read aloud the chant from the book.

Amy didn't recognize any of the words. They sounded like they belonged to another language.

As James spoke, the stones on the talismans began to glow. Amy watched, breathless, as the talismans lifted off of the ground and floated into the air.

James chanted faster, and the talismans began to swirl in circles. Then there was a bright, blinding flash of light. When Amy could see again, the talismans were gone.

"They're gone!" Amy said. "The spell must have worked. Diamanda can't use the talismans to hurt Bleaktown."

"There's only one way to know for sure," James said.

They walked back to the site of the Shadow Society headquarters, but the building was gone. In the middle of the empty space stood a tall man with black hair. He looked dazed.

"Uncle Marshall!" James cried.

James ran and hugged his uncle. Together, James and Amy told him how they had stolen the talismans and destroyed their power. Marshall explained that since the building had been created with the talismans, it had disappeared along with them.

"So Bleaktown is safe?" Amy asked.

Marshall nodded. "Thanks to you two. You guys are amazing."

Amy smiled. It definitely felt pretty amazing.

Amy and James stayed friends after that, and Amy never ate alone in the lunchroom again.

THE END

Continued from page 103

Amy wasn't sure how she managed it, but a scream erupted from somewhere deep inside her.

"Stoooooooooooooop!" she yelled.

In the next instant, several things happened.

Adam and the Shadow People vanished in a flash.

The necklace clattered onto the lunch table.

And every single person in the lunchroom stopped talking and stared at Amy.

Normally, Amy would have crawled under the table, dying of embarrassment, but she was too excited about getting rid of Adam and the Shadow People. Her cheeks blushed red, and she gave a little shrug. Then reality hit her.

Oh no, she worried. *They're going to laugh at me, or throw things at me . . .*

But no one did. They all turned back to their lunch and started talking again.

Everyone but Keesha, that is. She rushed over to Amy's table with a look of concern on her face.

"Amy, was that you? Are you all right?" she asked.

"I'm fine," Amy said. "I, uh, I saw a mouse! It really scared me."

Keesha shuddered. "Gross!" she said. "You should come eat lunch with us in case that mouse

116

comes back again."

Amy looked behind Keesha at the group of girls sitting at Keesha's table. Once, the idea of sitting with them had seemed scary.

Now it didn't seem so bad. At least they weren't see-through, like Adam and the Shadow People.

"Thanks," Amy said. "But first I need to go to the girls' room. I have to uh, check something."

"Sure thing," Keesha said, flashing a smile.

Amy slipped the necklace into her pocket. Then she locked herself in a bathroom stall and slowly lifted up the leg of her jeans. She had a hope, but there was only one way to find out.

"Yes!" Amy cried. Both of her legs were visible again. The magic was over. She wasn't sure how it had happened, but she guessed it probably had something to do with her crying out in the lunchroom. It's hard to be invisible when you're screaming at the top of your lungs.

"No more necklace," Amy muttered, as she headed back to grab her yogurt. She knew what she wanted to do with it. She was taking it back to Sebastian Cream right after school. His spooky shop was the only place for the necklace now.

Amy walked up to Keesha's table. Keesha pulled up a seat for Amy right next to her.

"Keesha said you saw a mouse," said one of the

girls. "That is, like, so disgusting! They should shut down this place—right, Amy?"

Amy smiled. Maybe living in the real world wasn't going to be so bad any more.

go to page 144

Don't be stupid, Amy, she scolded herself. *This necklace is the cause of all your problems. Don't use it again.*

Amy sat up. The door opened, and Keesha walked in.

"Are you okay, Amy?" she said. "You really scared me in the locker room."

"I'm fine," Amy said. "Really. It's just a little bump, that's all."

"Good!" Keesha said. "I'll see you later, okay?"

Amy nodded. "Thanks."

Keesha closed the door, and Amy leaned back on the cot. That hadn't been so bad after all.

Of course, she was still stuck with an invisible foot. Amy lifted up her pants leg and pulled down her sock.

Her foot had reappeared.

Amy stared at her foot in wonder. She blinked her eyes again and again, just to make sure it was true. But why had it become visible again?

"Maybe it's because I talked to Keesha, instead of hiding from her," Amy whispered. "Maybe I've been hiding from things for too long."

As Amy said the words, she felt a tingling in

119

her pocket. Amy pulled out the necklace. It was shimmering with a soft light.

And then it disappeared.

The nurse opened the door and stepped in. "Feeling better?" she asked.

Amy smiled. "Yeah," she replied. "Better than I've been feeling in a long time!"

THE END

Amy bolted from her bed and ran out of her room. Her feet thudded on the steps as she ran downstairs.

"Amy, is that you?" she heard her mother's voice behind her.

But Amy, in her panic, did not stop. She ran through the back door and into the yard.

Dumb move, Amy, she scolded herself. *Now there's nowhere to go.*

Amy spun around. The Shadow People were streaming out of her house, led by Adam. They floated toward her with eerie smiles on their faces.

Amy's mind raced. Then she realized that she still held the necklace tightly in her right hand. There was nowhere to run. Maybe using the necklace was the answer.

Adam led the Shadow People closer and closer.

"Don't be scared, Amy," he said.

Amy fumbled with the clasp of the necklace. Time seemed to move in slow motion as she fastened the necklace around her neck.

It worked. The Shadow People vanished. Amy let out a long breath. Then, still invisible, she snuck back up into her bedroom and took off the necklace. She was under the covers when her mom opened the door.

"Are you okay, Amy?" she asked. "I thought I heard you come downstairs."

"I'm fine, Mom," Amy answered. "Just fine."

And Amy did feel better. She had escaped the Shadow People, or whatever they were. That was a step. Tomorrow she'd start researching the necklace again.

The next morning, Amy was relieved to see that the invisibility hadn't spread any further. In school, Amy took her usual seat in the back of the room. Mr. Moore began to call attendance. Soon he got to the "I"s.

"Amy Izzo," he called out. "Has anyone seen Amy today?"

Amy raised her hand. "I'm here, Mr. Moore," she said.

But the teacher didn't seem to hear her.

"So Amy's not here," he said, making a check in his book.

Amy stood up. "Mr. Moore, I'm right here!" she said, as loud as she could.

Then Amy heard a chilling voice behind her.

"No, Amy." It was Adam. "You're in our world now."

Amy slowly turned around. Adam and the Shadow People were standing there, but now they looked solid. Amy's classmates were the ones who looked see-through.

"You got your wish, Amy," Adam said. "Now everyone will leave you alone."

"But I didn't really want that wish," Amy said, her voice rising in panic.

"But you put on the necklace, Amy," Adam said.

"It's not fair!" Amy screamed. "I was just trying to get away from you!"

Amy ran to Mr. Moore. "Help me!" she screamed. She reached out to grab his arm . . .

Her hand passed right through him, as though he wasn't there.

Amy stared at her hands in disbelief. When she looked up again, she saw Adam grinning at her.

"He can't help you, Amy," he said. "No one can help you now!"

THE END

Continued from page 54

Amy shook her head. "I'm sorry," she said. "This is all too weird. I can't help you. I don't even know who you are."

Billy's friendly expression changed to a scowl. His green eyes flashed.

"What do you mean, you won't help me?"

As Billy spoke, his voice got deeper and more distorted. Amy watched in horror as the ghostly boy transformed before her eyes. The cute freckled face was replaced with one that looked more animal than human.

"You should have helped me, Amy," Billy said. "I don't like it when people don't help me."

A green light shot from Billy's eyes, zapping Amy. The blast knocked the wind out of her.

Then Amy's body began to tingle. Her head felt light.

Then her world went dark.

When Amy opened her eyes, she found that she was in some kind of round room. The wall in front of her was like a giant window made of milky-white glass.

Amy stared out of the glass and gasped. There was her room, but it looked much, much, bigger than ever before. Either Billy had made her room larger, or else . . .

Amy started to panic as she the truth dawned on her. The room hadn't gotten bigger. She had become smaller.

And she wasn't in any room. She was trapped inside the stone of the necklace!

Amy screamed and pounded on the glass wall.

"Let me out!" she screamed.

Suddenly, Billy's huge face loomed in front of her. One of his eyeballs was larger than her whole body.

"Sorry, Amy," Billy said. "You should have helped me."

Then Billy vanished.

"No!" Amy wailed. "Come back! I'll help you!"

Amy screamed and pounded with all her might. Suddenly, a shadow loomed over the glass.

"You came back!" Amy said, relieved. "Just tell me what to do."

But as the figure got closer, Amy realized that it wasn't Billy. It was a little boy in a peanutbutter-stained shirt and a diaper.

"Mikey!" Amy cried. "It's me, Amy. Take me to Mommy, Mikey. That's a good boy."

Mikey picked up the necklace and studied it. Then he waddled out of the room.

Amy tried to stay calm. Her mom and dad would figure out how to get her out. This would all be over soon.

Mikey turned down the hallway and wobbled into the bathroom.

"Not here, Mikey," Amy yelled. "Take me to Mommy!"

Mikey walked to the toilet bowl and dangled the necklace over the water.

"Clean Amy," Mikey said.

Amy heard the sound of a flush.

"Noooooooooo!" she cried.

THE END

Continued from page 40

Amy took a deep breath.

"I'll help you," she told James. She held out the necklace. "I have one of the talismans. It turns you invisible. Maybe we could use it to find your uncle."

James's eyes widened. He reached out and touched the stone.

"I've never seen one up close before," he said. "Does it really work?"

Amy nodded. "I can show you."

Amy fastened the talisman around her neck. She heard James gasp as she became invisible.

"Wow!" he said. "That's amazing. Can I try it?"

Amy smiled for the first time in days. She almost forgot that they were in the basement of a mysterious building, trying to stop a society of weirdos from doing something terrible to their town. It just felt good to share the secret of the necklace with someone. She started to unclasp the necklace.

Then something caught her eye. There were shadowy figures on the far wall. They looked just like Adam had when he appeared to her at the school. The figures wore gray clothes.

"Someone's here!" Amy cried.

The members of the Shadow Society had seen Amy. They began to point. Amy quickly took off the necklace.

"I think we need to get out of here," she said. "I can't explain it, but when I put on the necklace, it's like the people in the society can see me. I think they know I'm in the basement."

James didn't ask questions. "Right. I know a quick way out. Let's go!"

Amy followed James through the dank basement and up a short flight of stairs. James opened a door overhead and they found themselves out on the street, in the bright sunlight. They took off running and didn't stop until they were blocks away.

James wanted to know more about Amy's necklace, so the two talked as they walked toward Amy's house. She told him the whole story, starting with her birthday party. It felt good to share what had happened with somebody.

James looked thoughtful as she talked. "I wonder why that necklace ended up with you," he said when she was finished. "It's pretty strange, isn't it?"

"I guess it is," Amy said. "I haven't really thought about it."

"Uncle Marshall says things always happen for a reason," James said. "Maybe you were meant to have the necklace somehow."

"Right," Amy said. They had reached the top of her block. "So what do we do now?"

"I was thinking about that," James said. "Maybe we should go back tonight. Uncle Marshall said the place was usually empty after nine o'clock. If they're keeping him there, we can find him."

Amy hesitated. Sneaking out at night was pretty dangerous.

Then Amy looked at the necklace in her hands. Somehow the fact that she had been given the necklace tied her into everything. It didn't feel right to stop things now. It was like she was in the middle of a story—and she wanted to find out what was supposed to happen.

She nodded. "I'll go with you."

"I'll meet you here at nine," James said.

When the time came, Amy knew she couldn't sneak out of the house without her parents seeing her. She pretended to go to bed early, then used the necklace for just a few minutes until she got outside.

James was waiting for her at the corner. He was carrying a small backpack.

"I brought some flashlights and tools and stuff," he said.

"And I've got the necklace," Amy said.

The two didn't say a word until they got to the gray building. James led Amy to the back, which faced a narrow alleyway and a high brick fence. James knelt down and pushed open a small window near the ground.

"This is how I get in," James said. "Come on."

Amy followed James and found they were once again in the basement, but in a different part. They seemed to be in a storage room of some kind.

James opened his pack and handed Amy a small flashlight.

"I've checked the basement already," he whispered. "My uncle's not down here. Let's check the first floor."

James led Amy to a nearby staircase. Slowly and quietly they crept up the stairs and opened the door that led them into a hallway. Amy counted six doors along the walls—that meant six rooms to explore.

The first three rooms were empty. When they tried the fourth door, it wouldn't open. James reached into his backpack and took out a small metal pick with a sharp point.

"Shine the flashlight on the lock," James instructed. Amy obeyed, and James inserted the pick into the lock.

"Uncle Marshall showed me how to do this,"

James whispered, holding his ear to the door. He moved the pick around for a few seconds, and then he smiled. The door swung right open.

Continued on page 92.

Continued from page 73

Amy slipped on her necklace. Then, invisible, she climbed under the velvet rope and grabbed the cube. She quickly stashed it in her backpack.

Amy climbed back out and took off the necklace.

"You'd better disappear," she told Billy. "We can check this out at home."

But it was hours later, after doing homework, eating dinner, and playing with Mikey, before Amy had a chance to take a close look at the cube. She took it out of her backpack and set it on her desk. Billy appeared next to her. Amy picked up the cube, turning it over in her hands.

The cube was made almost entirely of silver. On each side of the cube was embedded a round pendant with a white stone in the center—just like her necklace.

Then Amy noticed that one of the sides was missing a pendant. There was a round indentation where the pendant should be. She showed it to Billy.

"I wonder," she said thoughtfully. She held the necklace up to the empty spot. It looked like her pendant would fit perfectly.

Billy knew what she was thinking.

"Try it," he said.

Amy slipped the round pendant off of the chain. Then she pressed the pendant into the empty circle on the side of the cube.

The sides of the cube sprang open. A beam of pure white light shot up from to the ceiling. Billy stared at the light, transfixed. Then he floated up and into the light.

"Billy!" Amy cried. What was happening?

A huge smile broke out on Billy's face.

"There's my sister!" Billy cried. "And my dog! And my home! I'm going home! We did it, Amy!"

Then all at once the light faded and the sides of the box snapped closed. Amy stared, unable to move for what seemed like a long time. Then she reached out and took her pendant out of the cube.

She wore wear the necklace one last time—to return the cube to the museum. After that, she returned the pendant to its place on the cube. Amy's necklace—and the secret of the cube— remained safe in Agatha's drawing room for years after.

THE END

Continued from page 113

Amy had another idea. She handed the necklace to Billy.

"You wear it," she said. "Maybe that's the boost
that you need."

Billy clasped the necklace around his neck.

BOOM! A noise like thunder exploded in the
room. The air crackled with electricity.

And right before Amy's eyes, Billy's body started to become more and more solid.

Seconds later, all was silent. Billy stood in the
circle, just as solid and real as Amy.

"We did it!" Amy cried. She rushed into the
circle and hugged Billy.

"Amy, what on earth is going on here?" Mrs.
Izzo burst into the room holding Mikey in her
arms. Mr. Izzo stood behind her, rubbing sleep
from his eyes. "Who is this boy?"

Before Amy could answer, there was a loud
knock on the door.

"You two come downstairs right now," Mrs.
Izzo said. "I want an explanation!"

Mr. Izzo opened the door to reveal Amy's Aunt
Irene. Her purple nightgown peeked out from
under her coat, and her red hair frizzed out in all
directions.

"I had a dream," she said. "About Billy. That he was here."

Mr. Izzo put an arm around her and led her inside. "Aunt Irene, you know Billy's been missing for fifty years."

"But Dad," Amy said, "this is Billy. He's my friend."

Aunt Irene let out a scream and rushed toward Billy, picking him up and squeezing him tight.

"Billy! My little brother! I knew you'd come back!" she choked out between tears.

Billy looked into Irene's eyes. "Wow, it's you, Sis. You sure got big."

Amy suddenly realized the truth. Billy and Aunt Irene were brother and sister. He must have disappeared fifty years ago. And now he was back—thanks to the necklace.

"Amy, what is going on?" her mother asked.

Amy smiled. "It's a long story, Mom. A really long story."

THE END

Diamanda began chanting words in a strange language. The other members of the society joined in, and the chant grew louder. As they chanted faster and faster, the stones in the talismans began to glow.

Amy realized that the society was too busy chanting to pay any attention to her. If she was going to do something, now was the time.

It's now or never Amy, she told herself.

Then she jumped off of her chair.

"Stoooooooop!" she yelled, screaming like a wild woman. She wasn't sure why, but screaming seemed like a good thing to do.

Amy burst into the circle. The members were too startled to do anything at first. Amy charged at the pedestal and slammed into it, knocking the talismans to the floor.

"No!" Diamanda cried. "The spell cannot be disturbed!"

But it was too late. The stones in the talismans cracked, one by one. The strange glow vanished. Adam picked up the invisibility talisman. Pieces of the broken stone sifted through his fingers.

"This is all your fault!" Adam said, glaring at Amy. "Mother, can't we fix it?"

But Diamanda knelt on the ground, holding the other talismans and weeping.

"All our years of planning destroyed!" she wailed. "There is nothing we can do now!"

Suddenly, the Shadow Society didn't seem so scary to Amy anymore. They looked like a bunch of sad and lonely people. While they comforted Diamanda, Amy slipped out the door and found the nearest exit.

The sun was shining as she walked down the street. Amy felt better than she had in a long time. Not only was she free of the necklace, but she had saved Bleaktown, too. It wasn't the greatest town in the world—but it wasn't the worst one, either.

Amy had walked a few blocks, when she saw someone waving to her up ahead.

"Hey, Amy!" Keesha cried. "Where were you at lunch today?"

Amy walked up to her old friend. "Sorry," she said. She quickly thought up an excuse. "I had to go home for something."

"No problem," Keesha said. "Maybe tomorrow?"

Amy smiled. She had just faced a secret society intent on plunging Bleaktown into a shadow world. Maybe facing Keesha's friends wouldn't be so bad.

"Sure," Amy said, smiling. "Tomorrow."

THE END

Continued from page 91

Amy couldn't keep her eyes open any longer.

"Wake me up if you find something," she said, sinking into her pillow.

As Amy slept, she dreamed that her body was growing lighter and lighter until she floated off of the bed. It was such a strange sensation that she woke up.

Billy was standing next to her, wearing the necklace. He looked completely solid—like a real person.

"Billy!" she said, sitting up. "You figured it out! That's great!"

But a feeling of dread quickly replaced Amy's happiness. Something wasn't right. She looked down at her own body and saw that she was see-through—just like Billy used to be.

"Billy, what's happening?" she asked, her voice trembling. "Did something go wrong?"

Billy looked down at the carpet. "I'm sorry, Amy," he said. "I had to do it."

"Do what?" Amy jumped to her feet. Her heart pounded in her chest.

"The book said there was only one way for me to come back," he said. "I had to find someone to take my place in the Shadow World."

Amy looked down at her transparent body. "You mean . . ." she couldn't bear to say it.

Billy nodded. "I'm so sorry. I've been trapped in the Shadow World for ages. I couldn't take it anymore. You've got to understand!"

Billy took off the necklace and set it on the floor. Then he took a heavy bookend off of Amy's shelf.

"No!" Amy cried. "There has to be another way! Let's keep looking!"

"It has to be this way, Amy," Billy said.

Billy smashed the necklace with the bookend. Amy felt a strange, cold wind creep over her body.

Her bedroom vanished. Amy was standing in a shapeless void. Gray misty fog surrounded her on all sides.

"Nooooo!" Amy screamed, but there was no one to hear her.

She was trapped in the Shadow World forever.

THE END

Continued from page 93

"I'm not leaving you," Amy told James.

"It's no good if we're both caught," James said.

"I've got a better idea," Amy replied. She smacked the flashlight against the glass case. The lid smashed to pieces. Amy reached in and grabbed one of the talismans and the book. James followed her lead and grabbed the other talisman.

"Don't come any closer or we'll destroy them!" Amy yelled. She hoped she sounded convincing.

The two men in gray stopped and looked at Diamanda. Her blue eyes glittered with anger.

"You wouldn't dare," she said.

"Just watch me!" James shot back. He raised the talisman with the red stone above his head, as though he was going to throw it on the ground.

"No!" Diamanda cried, but at that very instant, a bright white light flashed from the red talisman. The next thing Amy knew, she and James were standing outside the building. It felt like a hundred bees were buzzing in Amy's head.

She heard James's voice through the buzz.

"That talisman must have transported us here," he said. "Let's go!"

For the second time that day, Amy and James found themselves running from the Shadow

Society. They didn't stop until they reached Amy's front steps.

"What next?" Amy asked.

"Diamanda knows Marshall is my uncle," James said. "She'll come after me. I don't think we have much time."

"She doesn't know who I am," Amy said. "Follow me. I know a place we can hide."

Amy led James to the potting shed in her backyard. The little shack was crowded with planters and huge bags of potting soil, but there was enough room for Amy and James to sit cross-legged on the floor. They placed the talismans between them. The white, red, and black stones glittered under the dim light of Amy's flashlight.

"What about the book?" Amy asked. "Maybe there's something that can help us in there."

James opened the cover and flipped through the brittle, yellowing pages.

"This is all about how the talismans were created," James said. "Man, they're old!"

"Does it say how to get rid of them?" Amy asked.

James frowned. "I'll keep looking."

Amy waited patiently while James looked through the book. Finally, he flashed a triumphant smile.

"Here it is!" he said. "It's some kind of spell of

something. It says, 'To Terminate the Power of the Talismans.'"

"That sounds right," Amy said. "If the talismans have no power, Diamanda can't use them, anyway. What do we do?"

"We're supposed to face east and read some kind of a chant," James said. "So which way is east?"

Amy thought. "Well, the sun rises in the east. We could see were the sun is."

"We could," James said, "but it's nighttime."

Amy blushed. "You're right. Maybe we can tell from the position of the moon."

They stepped outside the shed, but there was no moon visible in the sky.

"I know," James said. "I can see the tower of the Bleaktown Bank lit up over there, right? Well, I'm pretty sure the bank is on the east side of town."

"I don't know," Amy said. "I always thought the bank was on the west side of town."

"I know I'm right," James insisted. "Come on, let's try the spell!"

If Amy and James face the bank and say the spell, go to page 31.

If Amy and James have second thoughts, go to page 114.

Continued from several pages: 13, 118

Amy opened the door to Sebastian Cream's Junk Shop and stepped inside. She hadn't gone far when she bumped into a boy with dark hair.

"Sorry," he said. Amy realized it was Evan Kim, a sixth-grader from her school. He made a jangling noise when he stepped back. Amy saw that the sound came from the belt around his waist. All kinds of strange gadgets dangled from the belt. There was a flashlight, binoculars, and a bunch of other stuff Amy didn't recognize.

"Hi, Evan," Amy said, suddenly feeling self-conscious. "I'm, uh, just returning something."

Even nodded. "See you around."

Evan darted out the door, and Amy noticed that he carried a small paper bag. Amy took out her necklace and stared at it one last time.

The necklace had brought Amy plenty of excitement, that was true. But it also caused a lot of trouble. For a second, Amy wondered if Evan had something strange in store for him next.

Don't be silly, Amy scolded herself. *It's not like everything in this store has strange powers . . .*

THE END